P9-CCO-315

EYEWITNESS BOOKS

MEDIEVAL LIFE

Horn book

Writing quills

Horn inkwells

Papal ring

Church censer for burning incense

Carved wooden angel from a medieval church nave

Medieval stone carving of a woman's head

Shepherd's horn pipe

12th-century reliquary casket

Bagpipes

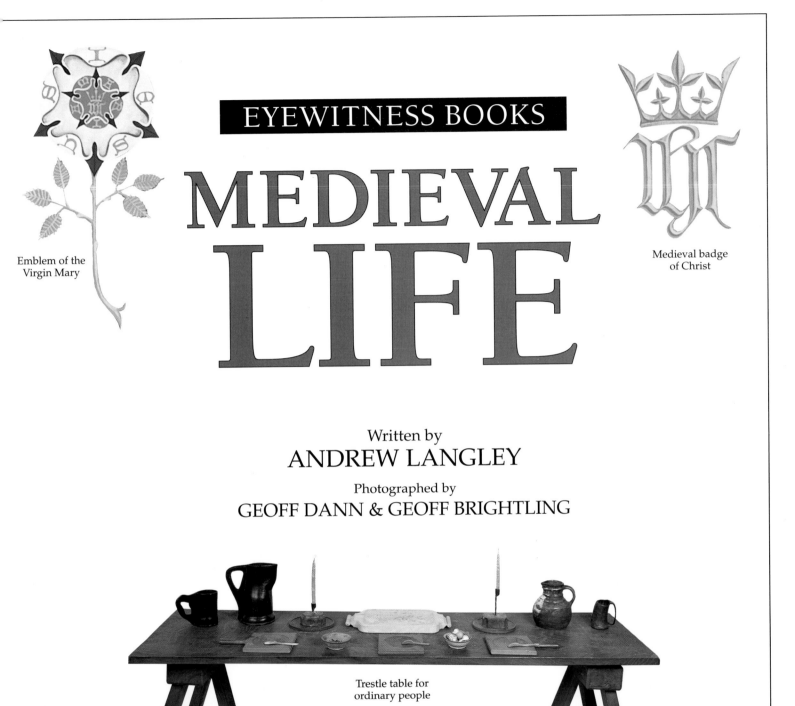

Emblem of the
Virgin Mary

Medieval badge
of Christ

EYEWITNESS BOOKS

MEDIEVAL LIFE

Written by
ANDREW LANGLEY

Photographed by
GEOFF DANN & GEOFF BRIGHTLING

Trestle table for
ordinary people

Conard High School Library
West Hartford, Conn.

ALFRED A. KNOPF • NEW YORK

Harp

Shawm, or
medieval reed
instrument

Spoons
cut from
horn

A DORLING KINDERSLEY BOOK

Project editor Bridget Hopkinson
Art editor Vicky Wharton
Designer Kati Poynor
Managing editor Gillian Denton
Managing art editor Julia Harris
Researcher Céline Carez
Production Charlotte Trail
Picture research Kathy Lockley
Consultants Peter Brears, Charles Kightly

This is a Borzoi Book published by Alfred A. Knopf, Inc.

This Eyewitness ™ Book has been conceived by
Dorling Kindersley Limited and Editions Gallimard

First American edition, 1996

Copyright © 1996 by Dorling Kindersley Limited, London. All
rights reserved under International and Pan-American Copyright
Conventions. Published in the United States by Alfred A. Knopf,
Inc., New York. Distributed by Random House, Inc., New York.
Published in Great Britain by Dorling Kindersley Limited,
London, in 1996.

101919

Manufactured in Singapore
0 9 8 7 6 5 4 3 2

Library of Congress Cataloging-in-Publication Data
Langley, Andrew.
Medieval life / written by Andrew E. Langley; photographed by
Geoff Brightling & Geoff Dann.
p. cm. — (Eyewitness books)
Includes index.
Summary: An illustrated look at various aspects of life in
medieval Europe, covering everyday life, religion, royalty, and
more.
ISBN 0-679-88077-1 (trade). — ISBN 0-679-98077-8 (lib. bdg.)
1. Civilization, Medieval—Juvenile literature. [1. Civilization,
Medieval. 2. Middle Ages.]
I. Brightling, Geoff, ill. II. Dann, Geoff, ill. III. Title.
CB35 1.L34 1996
940.1—dc20   95-25064

series

940.1
LAN

Color reproduction by
Colourscan, Singapore
Printed in Singapore
by Toppan

Stone carving of a man
"pulling a face"

"Back" stool

Drinking
vessel

Table setting

Spoons
cut from
horn

Decorated
ceramic jugs
for wine or ale

Wooden food
bowl

Contents

Tester bed

The Middle Ages

THE TERM "MEDIEVAL" COMES from the Latin *medium aevum*, which means "the middle ages." But when were the Middle Ages? Before them came the Classical Age of ancient Greece and Rome, and after them came the Renaissance (p. 62). The Middle Ages covered the period roughly in between, from the fifth century to the end of the 15th. In many ways medieval times seem remote and mysterious, peopled by knights and ladies, kings and bishops, monks and pilgrims. Yet European cities, states, parliaments, banking systems, and universities all had their roots there, and parts of the landscape are still dominated by the great medieval castles and cathedrals.

A LIGHT IN THE DARK
During the Dark Ages, art and learning survived in remote monasteries. This illuminated letter comes from the *Book of Kells* (c. 800), which was kept at St. Columba's monastery in Ireland.

THE BYZANTINE EMPIRE
When the Roman Empire split in two, the western half, based in Rome, declined, but the eastern half, based in the Byzantine capital of Constantinople, flourished. Its greatest ruler was the Christian emperor Justinian I (c. 482–565).

Viking brooches

SEA RAIDERS
The Vikings began to raid the coasts of Europe toward the end of the eighth century.

KING OF EUROPE
Charles the Great, or Charlemagne (742–814), united an empire covering much of modern France and Germany. He was a great Christian leader as well as a skillful warrior.

OTTO THE GREAT
The Magyar tribes that flooded into Europe in the tenth century were stopped by the German king Otto I (912–973). He became Charlemagne's successor when the Pope made him Holy Roman Emperor in 962. His realm in western Europe became known as the Holy Roman Empire.

THE DARK AGES
In the fifth century, the Roman Empire slowly fell apart as Germanic tribes from the north pushed across its frontiers, destroying towns and trade routes. Saxons settled in Britain, Franks took over Gaul (France), and Goths invaded Italy itself. In 476, the last Roman emperor lost his throne. These centuries of disorder became known as the "Dark" Ages, but this was not an entirely accurate description. Under the sixth-century emperor Justinian I, the Byzantine capital of Constantinople became one of the most magnificent cities in the world. By the eighth century, the great Frankish ruler Charlemagne had once more united a large part of Europe, encouraging the spread of learning and Christianity throughout his empire.

THE GREAT LEADERS
The Christian king Charlemagne supported the Pope as he tried to drive the barbarian invaders out of Italy, and in 800 the Pope crowned him "Holy Roman Emperor" in gratitude. Europe was threatened by invaders throughout the ninth and tenth centuries – Vikings raided the northern coasts, and the fierce Magyars pressed in from central Asia. But gradually new nations began to emerge. The lands of the Franks became France, Alfred the Great (871–899) defeated the Vikings to become king of England, and Otto I of Germany fought off the Magyars.

400–800

800–1000

NORMANS NORTH AND SOUTH
As William of Normandy (c. 1027–1087) was conquering England in 1066, other Norman nobles were carving out a large empire in Italy and Sicily.

THE CRUSADES
The Crusades (p. 28) began in 1095 as a Christian campaign to drive the Muslims out of the Holy Land. Jerusalem was captured in 1099, but later crusades were less successful.

German crusader's helmet

THE GREAT PLAGUE
The Black Death had a lasting effect on European society. So many peasants died that there were hardly enough people left to farm the land. Increased demands on their labor caused the peasants to revolt in both France and England.

UNIFIER
This beautiful gilded head represents the powerful Holy Roman emperor Frederick I, or Barbarossa (1121–90), who brought unity to the German states in the 12th century.

Bishop's crozier, or crook

THE CHURCH
The Catholic Church was one of the most powerful institutions of the Middle Ages. During the 13th century, the religious Inquisition was established to hunt out those who disagreed with its teachings. Those found guilty could be punished with excommunication (being cut off from the Church) or even death.

RENAISSANCE GENIUS
Michelangelo (1475–1564) was one of the greatest Renaissance sculptors. His most famous work is the beautiful marble statue the *David*, now in Florence.

DISSOLVING THE MONASTERIES
When the English king Henry VIII (1491–1547) quarreled with the Catholic Church, he appointed himself head of the Church in England and "dissolved" the great monasteries, taking their lands and property.

PEACE AND STABILITY
After 1000, life in Europe became more stable. Supported by the feudal system (p. 8), strong rulers brought order and peace to the new nations. This encouraged trade and the growth of towns and cities, and the population rose. The Catholic Church (p. 30) reached the peak of its power as great cathedrals were built and new monastic orders were formed (p. 36). The first European university was founded in Italy.

PLAGUE AND WAR
The 14th century saw a series of disasters strike Europe. Bad harvests caused famine, and the Black Death (p. 60) killed a third of the population. England and France began the Hundred Years' War in 1337, and church leaders squabbled over the title of pope. However, there was also an expansion in trade spearheaded in northern Europe by the prosperous Hanseatic League (p. 47).

NEW BEGINNINGS
The 15th century was a time of change. Scholars and artists explored new ideas and artistic styles in the Renaissance (p. 62), and in the 1500s religious reformers broke away from the Catholic Church in the Reformation (p. 62). This was also an age of great discovery. Explorers from Spain and Portugal crossed the Atlantic and Indian oceans, opening new horizons for trade and development (p. 63).

1000–1250

1250–1400

1400–1540

Medieval society

TOP OF THE TREE
In this 14th-century picture, a French king presides over a gathering of his most important vassals, with the bishops on one side and barons on the other.

GOD'S DEPUTY
Medieval kings were seen as God's deputies on earth. A coronation was a magnificent religious ceremony; archbishops anointed the new king with holy oil as a sign of his status.

SOCIETY IN MUCH OF medieval Europe was organized into a "feudal" system, which was based on the allocation of land in return for services. The king gave fiefs, or grants of land, to his most important noblemen (barons and bishops), and in return, each noble promised to supply the king with soldiers in time of war. A noble pledged himself to be the king's vassal, or servant, at a special ceremony – kneeling before the king, he swore an oath of loyalty with the words "Sire, I become your man." The great nobles often divided their lands among lower lords, or knights, who in turn became their vassals. In this way, feudalism stretched from the top to the bottom of society. At the very bottom were the peasants who worked the land itself. They had few rights, little property – and no vassals.

TAXES NOT AXES
By about 1100, many vassals were unwilling to fight for their king. Instead, they were allowed to pay a sum of cash, called "scutage," or shield money, which could be used to hire soldiers. Scutage was one of the first regular money taxes levied by kings from their noblemen. A system of tax collectors (above) made sure that the full amounts were paid.

THE PEASANTS
The peasants were at the bottom of the feudal tree. They were the workers who farmed the land to provide food for everyone else. Most peasants worked for a lord who let them farm a piece of land for themselves in return for their labor (p. 10).

THE LORDS
Lords ruled over fiefs or manors (p. 14), renting out most of their land to the peasants who worked for them. They were also the warriors of medieval society. As trained knights, they were bound by oath to serve the great nobles who granted them their fiefs, and they could be called to battle at any time.

THE BARONS
Barons (p. 24) were the most powerful and wealthy noblemen, and received their fiefs directly from the king. When William of Normandy (p. 7) conquered England in 1066, he had about 120 barons. Each provided him with a possible army of over 5,000 men.

Bishop wears a miter (p. 31) as a sign of his status

King is mockingly portrayed with a cat on his head!

THE BISHOPS

Bishops often wielded as much power as the barons. They ruled over areas called dioceses (p. 31) and all the priests and monasteries within them. The regular collection of tithes (p. 13) and other taxes from their dioceses made many bishops extremely rich.

THE KING

Few kings had enough wealth to keep a standing army and depended on their barons to provide knights and soldiers. But kings had to work hard to keep their barons under control (p. 26). In many cases, especially in France and Germany, the great barons grew very powerful and governed their fiefs as independent states.

ROUGH JUSTICE

In the Middle Ages, ordinary people had few rights. Those who broke the law were tried in the court of their lord, who had almost complete power over them. Punishment for crimes was often harsh – a convicted criminal might be dragged behind a horse, whipped, locked in the stocks, or hanged, depending on the nature of his or her crime. But being at the top of the feudal system did not always ensure better treatment. Lords and barons sometimes had to pay their king large sums of money to get a fair trial. The medieval Church operated its own justice system with its own laws (the canon laws) and courts (p. 31) that were outside the jurisdiction of the king.

A peasant's life

Statue of a French peasant, c. 1500

ACCORDING TO THE LAW, medieval peasants did not belong to themselves. Everything, including their land, their animals, their homes, their clothes, and even their food, belonged to the lord of the manor (p. 14). Known as serfs or villeins, peasants were bound to work for their lord, who allowed them to farm their own piece of land in return. Their lives were ones of almost constant toil. Most struggled to produce enough food to feed their families as well as to fulfill their duties to the lord. Forbidden from leaving the manor without permission, the only way for a peasant to gain freedom was by saving enough money to buy a plot of land, or by marrying a free person.

Simple spoons can be cut from horn

Shepherd's horn pipe

DAILY GRIND
Peasants worked hard every day except Sundays and holy days, in blazing sun, rain, or snow. Combined with a poor diet, it isn't surprising that the average European peasant in 1300 lived no longer than 25 years.

Tired peasant wipes the sweat from his brow

DO IT YOURSELF
Peasants made some of their own tools and utensils, although skilled craftsmen produced their pottery, leatherwork, and iron. Besides wood and leather, the most important material was horn from cattle or sheep. Light and strong, it did not absorb flavors like wood and did not require great energy to shape (p. 16). Horn spoons were easy to clean, according to one writer: "With a little licking they will always be kept as clean as a die."

THE PEASANTS' REVOLT
After the Black Death (pp. 60–61), there was a shortage of labor in 14th-century Europe. The peasants had to work harder than ever, and in England they also had to pay an extra tax. In 1381, the English peasants rose in rebellion. Led by Wat Tyler, they marched on London, where they murdered the archbishop. When they met the king, Richard II (1367–1400), he agreed to end the new tax, but Wat Tyler was killed in a quarrel. The peasant mob swiftly disbanded and went home. The French Jacquerie revolt of 1358 ended much more bloodily when armored knights slaughtered several thousand rebels.

Straw hat to protect the head on hot days

Cheap pewter badge for good luck

Felt hat decorated with a cockerel feather and a "fleur-de-lis" badge

Brown woolen jacket lined with linen

Blue woolen doublet fastened with "points"

Linen shirt

Linen underpants, or braes

Leather flask, or costrel, for carrying ale into the fields

Peasants working with their hose rolled up

Woolen "split" hose can be rolled down for working

PEASANT COTTAGE
Most peasants lived in simple homes like this reconstructed 13th-century cottage. The walls are made from local flint, but they were more often made from wattle and daub – woven strips of wood covered with a mixture of dung, straw, and clay. Inside, the floor was bare, trampled earth. Most cottages had only one or two rooms, which contained basic furniture such as a trestle table and bench, a chest for clothes, and straw mattresses to sleep on. There was a stone hearth in the center of the main room, but no chimney, so it must have been very dark and smoky.

Leather working boots

PLAIN CLOTHES
These are the kind of clothes that would have been worn by a peasant in the 1440s. Clothes, like tools, were mostly homemade from local materials. Peasant women spent much of their time spinning wool into coarse thread, which was then woven into cloth and made into garments. Sheepskin cloaks were worn in winter to keep out the cold and rain, and wooden pattens (p. 23) could be put on over leather boots in muddy conditions. Although outer clothes were never washed, linen underwear was laundered regularly. People's clothes generally smelled of wood smoke, which had a deodorizing effect!

Tied to the soil

IN MEDIEVAL EUROPE, more than 90 percent of the population lived and worked on the land. Farming was a full-time job, since methods were ancient and not very efficient. The crop-growing areas around a village were usually divided into three big fields. Peasants were allotted some land in each so that good and bad soil was shared out equally. They hoed and harvested their own strips, or plots, but worked together on big jobs such as plowing and hay-making. A failed harvest could mean starvation for the whole village.

Wooden pitchfork for lifting hay and wheat sheaves

Man knocking acorns out of an oak tree for his pigs

Seeds fell in the plowed furrows, but many were lost to hungry birds

Farmer broadcasts the seeds in a sweeping arc

HARVEST-TIME
In late summer, women and children worked alongside the men to bring in the harvest. They cut the wheat with sickles, grasping each clump firmly so that the grains wouldn't shake loose. The wheat was then tied in sheaves, or bundles, set in stooks, or shocks, in the field to ripen, loaded onto a cart, and taken to the barn. Once the harvest was in, the wheat was threshed – beaten with a flail, or hinged stick, to loosen the grains from the ears.

SOWING THE SEED
In the "three-field system," two fields were sown with crops in one year while the third was left fallow, or empty, so it could recover its strength. One field was sown with wheat in winter, and the next spring, the second was sown with rye, barley, or oats. Seeds were broadcast, or scattered, by hand.

Basket of seeds called a seedlip

Shafts for pulling the cart

AUTUMN ACORNS
Every autumn, the lord of the manor allowed his serfs to run their pigs in his private woods, where they could feed on acorns and beechnuts. Sheep, geese, and goats grazed on common wasteland at the edge of the village. Even so, most animals were thin and wiry.

Hungry pig

Peasants working together at harvest-time

SHEAR PROFIT
Sheep shearing was the most important spring job in hilly regions of medieval Europe. Wool fetched high prices, and its trade became one of the richest industries of the Middle Ages.

TITHE BARN
This huge 13th-century barn was used to store tithes. Villagers had to give the local priest a tithe, or tenth, of everything they produced, from crops and firewood to eggs and flour. Tithes made some churches very wealthy – and very unpopular.

MANUAL LABOR
With no machines, all farm work was done by hand using simple tools like these. Most jobs involved back-breaking labor, from breaking clods (lumps of soil) to hoeing young crops.

Billhook for maintaining hedges

Sickle for harvesting crops

Threshed wheat stalks, or straw

Rear gate is tied to keep the straw from falling out

Rim of wooden wheel is clad with six iron strakes for extra strength

CARTED OFF
Medieval peasants would have transported their wheat, straw, and hay in carts like this. Straw (the leftover stalks from the harvest) was used for numerous purposes, from thatching roofs to making mattresses. Hay was another important crop. Along with wheat straw and dried beans, it provided the only winter feed for farm animals. Even then, there was rarely enough for all, and most cattle, pigs, and goats had to be killed in late autumn. Every peasant had a share in the village's hay meadow, and hay-making was a communal task.

Large wheels allow the cart to ride over big bumps and ruts

Running a manor

MOST COUNTRY PEOPLE LIVED on a manor, which consisted of a village, the lord's house or castle, a church, and the surrounding farmland. The lord of the manor governed the community and appointed officials who made sure that the villagers carried out their duties. These involved farming the demesne, or lord's land, and paying rents in the form of produce. The lord also acted as a judge in the manor court and had the power to fine those who broke the law. Since manors were often isolated, the villagers had to produce everything they needed themselves. Few goods, except salt for curing meat and iron for tools, came from outside. The only visitors were peddlers, pilgrims, or soldiers, and few people ever traveled far from their own village.

OTHER DUTIES
The lord was, first and foremost, a knight (p. 8) who provided arms for the king whenever he needed them. These knights are receiving their swords.

THE STEWARD
The lord left the daily running of his manor to a number of officials. The most important was the steward, who organized farmwork, kept accounts of the estate's money, and presided at the manor court if his master was away. Stewards were well-paid, powerful figures in the district.

Medieval watering pot

THE LORD AND LADY
The lord and lady of the manor had to oversee the running of the estate and their household, but they also had plenty of free time to pursue leisure activities. This French tapestry shows two angels holding a canopy over the heads of a noble and his lady, perhaps symbolizing their charmed lives!

THE MANOR HOUSE
The lord and his family lived in a large house, that was often built of stone. It was surrounded by gardens and stables, and was protected by a high wall and sometimes by a moat. Apart from church activities, the manor house was the center of community life – its great hall served as the manor court and as the venue for special village feasts, such as those given after the harvest and at Christmastime.

Favorite hawks were carried everywhere, even into church!

HAPPY HUNTING

Lords and ladies spent much of their time hunting, which was considered a noble pursuit. Many kept hawks to fly after rabbits or doves, and packs of hounds to chase deer or wild boar in their private woodlands.

GOING TO THE MILL

In most communities, there was only one watermill, which was owned by the lord. All other mills were often outlawed, so that the villagers were forced to use his mill for grinding their grain into flour. As payment, the lord kept some of their grain. Villagers might also have to bake their bread in the lord's oven and use his wine press for their grapes, for which they paid similar fees.

THE BAILIFF

Next in importance to the steward was the bailiff. He was usually a peasant, which can be seen from his clothes – they were made from better material than those of a farm laborer, but were basically the same style. However, the bailiff was not a serf (p. 10), but a freeholder who owned his own land. He was in charge of giving jobs to the peasants, looking after the demesne's cattle, and taking care of repairs to buildings and tools, for which he hired skilled craftsmen such as carpenters and smiths.

Peak keeps the sun out of the eyes and, when reversed, allows rainwater to run off

Felt hat

Brown doublet, or jacket

Woolen, linen-lined jacket with pewter buttons

Jacket was longer than that of a laborer

THE REEVE

The reeve was the bailiff's right-hand man. He was a peasant, chosen by the other villagers. Carrying a white stick as a badge of office, the reeve supervised work on the lord's demesne, checking that everyone began on time, and ensuring that none of the produce was stolen.

Stirrups pulled the hose closer to the leg for a fashionably slender look

Leather boots

15

A medieval home

MEDIEVAL HOMES WERE VERY DIFFERENT from ours. Peasants spent most of the daylight hours outside, so the drafts and little light from their unglazed windows did not trouble them. Inside, they kept below the smoke of the fire by sitting on low stools. For lighting, they peeled field rushes and dipped them in fat, which burned like small candles. Everything was kept as clean as possible – the earthen floors were often worn hollow as a result of constant sweeping. Domestic life was much more communal than ours, with whole families eating, sleeping, and spending free time together in their one- or two-roomed houses (p. 11). The homes of the wealthy were much more elaborate. By the 13th century, some noblemen had a private family room, called the solar. They paved their floors with decorated tiles and hung bright tapestries on their walls.

KEEPING WARM
Medieval homes had hearths in the center of the room – away from wooden walls to avoid the risk of fire. By the 1400s, more people could afford stone chimneys, so fireplaces were more common.

Shutters are closed at night

WINDOW ON THE WORLD
It was possible to judge the social status of a household by looking at its windows. The poor had small holes covered with wooden shutters that were closed at night or in cold weather. The better-off might have fenestral windows – lattice frames covered in linen that had been soaked in resin and tallow. These let in light and kept out drafts and could be removed on fine days.

Unwound horn

Central part is split and polished

Curly sheep's horn

HORN OF PLENTY
Horn has been called the plastic of the Middle Ages because it was cheap and pliable. To make a horn windowpane, the horn was first softened in water for three months, then unwound, split, and polished until it was transparent.

Urinal; urine was often saved to be used for cloth finishing and in dyeing processes

Wattle-and-daub wall (p. 11)

Some castle toilets emptied directly into the moat!

THE SMALLEST ROOM
By the late 15th century, many houses had an indoor toilet. It was little more than a closet in the wall with a hole over a cesspit. There probably would have been an outdoor toilet as well.

Horn panes are slotted into a wooden window frame

GLASS SUBSTITUTE
In the Middle Ages, glass was rare and expensive, and only churches or royal palaces could afford glass windows. Noblemen and merchants often made do with windows made from panes of polished horn. These were cheaper and tougher than glass and let in lots of light, although they were difficult to see through.

ROCK-A-BYE, BABY
This noble baby's rocking cradle was probably the most comfortable bed in the house. However, babyhood was a dangerous time – more than one-third of the infants died, usually from disease.

Cradle can be rocked by mother's foot while she sews or spins

SEATS TO SUIT
In most homes, people sat on plain stools or benches. Only a lord was likely to have a chair with a back and armrests, and he was thus called the "chairman."

Canopy is attached to the ceiling

BEDTIME
A 15th-century servants' book gives strict instructions on putting the lord to bed. After undressing him, combing his hair, and pulling on his nightcap, the servant should, "draw the curtains round about the bed, set there his night-light, drive out the dog and cat, giving them a clout, take no leave of your lord, but bow low to him and retire."

White rose of the Virgin Mary; many decorations bore religious symbols

Tester, or canopy

HANGINGS
Painted linen, woven tapestries, and fine wool cloths were hung from walls and doorways. They made rooms warmer by keeping out drafts, and added brightness to dim interiors. This doorway and painted linen wall-hanging come from the home of a wealthy merchant.

Warm woolen curtains keep out drafts

Linen pillow stuffed with chopped straw

Linen sheet

Woven straw mattress

"Truckle" bed was wheeled out for children, servants, and others to sleep on

Lavender   *Tansy*   *Ladies' bedstraw*

Woolen blanket

KEEPING BUGS AT BAY
Herbs such as lavender, tansy, and ladies' bedstraw were strewn on straw mattresses. Their strong scents not only made the bed smell sweeter, but also kept away fleas.

A ROOM WITHIN A ROOM
Wealthier people slept in beds made from strong timber beams, with a canopy overhead and curtains at the sides. The rich may have had feather-filled mattresses, but most were made of straw. When the curtains were drawn, the bed became a snug, private space. This bed would have belonged to a bailiff (p. 15) in the late 15th or early 16th century.

From kitchen to table

PEOPLE'S DIETS in the Middle Ages varied according to their means. Rich noblemen and merchants could afford to eat a wide range of food (p. 20) including expensive dried fruits, almonds, and spices from Asia. Although one poet believed the poor should live on "nettles, reeds, briars, and peashells," their diet was generally better than that. Ordinary people ate dark, coarse bread made from wheat mixed with rye or oatmeal, garden vegetables, and meat, especially pork, from their livestock. During the winter, they had to make do with meat and fish that had been preserved in salt, and cooks devised clever ways of masking the taste by adding oatmeal, peas, beans, or breadcrumbs to the pot. Cows, sheep, and goats provided milk for dairy foods, which were known as "white meats."

Small pot-hanger

Adjustable ratchet

Large pot-hook for a huge cauldron

Flesh-hook for removing meat from a boiling cauldron

Fresh river trout

HOOKS FOR COOKS
Most people boiled their food in iron pots that either hung from hooks over the fire or stood in the hot ashes. Once cooked, chunks of meat were pulled out of the pot with a flesh-hook. Vegetables and grains were added to the leftover liquid to make a soupy "pottage," which was a staple part of everyone's diet. This could be turned into thick pudding called frumenty by mixing it with wheat, crushed almonds, and egg yolks.

FAST FOOD
The Church ordered that Wednesdays, Fridays, and Saturdays were "fast" days, when no meat should be eaten. Fish was allowed and became a vital part of the diet. Ordinary people ate mainly salted or pickled herring, fresh eels, and shellfish. The wealthy could eat carp and pike from their fishponds and a wide variety of river and sea fish.

Pot-hook is suspended from an adjustable pot-hanger to allow the cauldron to be raised or lowered into the fire

Trivet, or pot stand

Stone hearth

Firewood

Three-legged cauldron can stand in the fire or hang from a pot-hook

Coneys, or rabbits, were a common source of fresh meat for ordinary people

A goose was often fattened for a special occasion

Wood pigeons could be wrapped in clay and baked in hot ashes

HEAD COOK
In a peasant household, the wife prepared the family's food, simmering pottage on the fire and baking bread on a hot stone. In manor or castle kitchens, the head cooks were always men. They roasted, broiled, and baked vast quantities of food in great fireplaces and ovens. A small army of scullions, or kitchen boys, were responsible for the dish washing.

Meat prepared on a chopping board

IN THE LARDER
Flesh larders, or pantries, were hung with all kinds of birds and beasts. Besides mutton, beef, and pork, there was rabbit, duck, pigeon, venison, and wild boar. No bird was safe from the hunter – everything, from swans and herons to blackbirds, was caught for the kitchen.

Rosemary

Sage

Mint

Parsley

A HANDFUL OF HERBS
Flavoring herbs were widely used in the Middle Ages to give interesting tastes to food that was often dull or salty. Vegetables such as turnips, leeks, onions, and cabbages were also known as "pot-herbs." Not regarded as food in their own right, they were thrown into the pot to fill out soups and stews.

"Fire dogs" support the blazing logs

Fork and poker for tending fire

Kindling

ON THE HEARTH
Wattle-and-daub peasant cottages (p. 11) had no chimneys, so cooking was done on a simple stone hearth in the center of the room. Great castles and manor houses had much bigger fireplaces with huge stone chimneys where meat could be roasted on spits. The fires in the English King John's (1167–1216) kitchens were large enough to roast two whole oxen at the same time. Since they posed a serious fire hazard, kitchens were housed in separate buildings away from the main hall.

Curfew (from the French couvre le feu) to cover the embers at night

High table, low table

Dinner was the grandest and biggest meal of the day. The lord of the manor sat with his most important guests at the "high" table, raised on a dais, or platform, at one end of the great hall. From here, he could look down on the lesser diners and members of his household sitting at the "low" tables. A feast might have three courses of cooked meats and fish, elaborate roasts of swans and peacocks re-clothed in their skins, followed by numerous sweet and spicy dishes. All of these were quickly carried from the nearby kitchen so that they arrived piping hot. The lord was served first, after a sample of the food had been tasted by a servant to make sure it was not poisoned. Only then were the other diners served.

Drinking vessel

Personal knife engraved with owner's initials

Square pewter trencher base used as a personal chopping board

Spoon was provided by the house

Wooden bowl for pottage

GET SET
In the Middle Ages, table forks did not exist, but everyone used their own knife, a spoon, strips of bread, and their fingers to eat very politely, for table manners were important and formed part of every wealthy child's education.

ENTERTAINING IN STYLE
At the high table, the lord sat on a bench at the center with his back to the wall. Guests were seated in order of importance, starting with churchmen, then noblemen, then the lord's family. Servants scurried to and fro with meats, sauces, and jugs of wine from the buttery (bottlery). Singers and acrobats often entertained the diners between courses.

The lord's seat at the center of the table

Expensive tiled floor

High table stood on a raised platform called a dais

Large jug for ale

Large wooden platter for serving bread or meat

Horn mug

Leather tankard

Spoons were placed facedown to "keep out the devil"

Trestle table

Hard wooden bench

BANQUET BUSTLE

The banqueting hall could be a crowded, noisy, smelly place. Tables were crammed with diners, and dogs crunched bones on the floor. Only the lord got a serving to himself. Other diners shared a bowl with up to three fellow guests. Most ate with their fingers, so it was important that these were clean and not used for blowing noses or scratching. Table etiquette was strict: "If it happen that you cannot help scratching," one writer advised, "then courteously take a portion of your dress, and scratch with that."

COMMON FARE

Diners seated at a low table would have eaten less elaborate food than that served up for the lord, but there were some common foods. Pottage, a thick broth of vegetables and meat stock, was a staple, everyday dish often served as a first course at feasts. Apart from pottage, everyone ate bread. All food was served on thick slices of stale bread called trenchers, and small loaves called manchets were used for mopping up gravy.

Expensive wine glass

Wooden drinking bowl

Glazed ceramic drinking vessel

Decorated ceramic jug for wine or ale

"Double-salt" for salt and mustard

Dyed cloth wall-cover

Linen tablecloth was "ironed" while damp using round glass linen smoothers

LAID FOR A LORD

The high table was carefully set out with a clean linen tablecloth, trencher bases, pottage and drinking bowls, salt, jugs, and, if the household was wealthy, fine glasses. In the 15th century, a large communal napkin called the long towel was spread over the knees of the diners once they were seated.

Medieval women

KEEP IT COVERED
Although young single women often wore their hair loose, married women were expected to keep their hair covered in a linen "wimple" as a sign of modesty.

"IT IS CLEAR," wrote a French priest in 1386, "that man is much nobler than woman, and of greater virtue." The medieval Church looked on women as inferior to men and taught that they should be meek and obedient to their fathers and husbands. But the real lives of women in the Middle Ages were rather different. Not all of them stayed quietly at home; most had to work for a living. Peasant women toiled alongside their husbands in the fields as well as having to feed and clothe their families. The wives and daughters of craftsmen were often employed in the workshop and frequently operated as tradeswomen in their own right. Wealthy ladies organized large households and sometimes ran their husbands' affairs. However, only a few powerful abbesses, noblewomen, and queens had any influence on national events.

THE MAID OF ORLEANS
St. Joan (1412–1431) was a French peasant's daughter who, at the age of 13, heard voices telling her to drive the invading English army out of France. Dressed in armor, she led the French troops to a great victory at the besieged town of Orleans. However, Joan was later betrayed and sold to the English, who burned her as a witch.

GET THEE TO A NUNNERY
Many unmarried gentlewomen entered convents and nunneries, where they lived lives similar to those of monks (pp. 36–39). Nunneries offered women the opportunity to lead a devout life and also to obtain an education and take on responsibilities denied them in the outside world. As local landowners and employers, many abbesses were important figures in the community (above).

HOLDING THE FORT
This noblewoman has collapsed on hearing of her husband's death. Many women took on the responsibility of running large estates when their husbands died in battle or were away at court or on a crusade (p. 28). They settled local disputes, managed the farms, and handled finances. Some women even fought battles, defending their castles when they were under siege.

WOMEN OF WEALTH
Landowners, male or female, were powerful figures in medieval society, and an unmarried woman of property had equal legal rights with men. She could make a will, and sign documents with her own seal – this 13th-century seal belonged to a French noblewoman called Elizabeth of Sevorc. However, when a woman married, she forfeited her land and rights to her husband. On his death she was entitled to a third of his land with which to support herself.

SPINSTERS
Spinning was done almost entirely by women using hand-held spindles like this one (the spinning wheel was introduced from India in the 13th century). Many single women earned a living in this way, hence the term "spinster" for an unmarried woman.

Wool twists into thread as the spindle twirls

WRAP–UP
Most women covered their hair with white linen head-wraps, but the wealthy wore gold nets over their coiled braids. The well-known pointed hat called the hennin was only popular for a short time in the late 15th century.

Linen head-wrap keeps hair clean as well as hidden

Decorated hairpins

Linen shift

AN EARLY FEMINIST
Christine de Pisan (1364–1429) was one of the few medieval women to earn a living by writing. She wrote poetry and books protesting the way women were both glorified and insulted by male authors.

Prayer beads

Pin-on sleeves worn on Sundays and special occasions

THE TOWNSWOMAN
A middle-class townswoman might have worn these clothes in the 15th century. In the towns, women worked in a variety of occupations. They might be shopkeepers, spinners, bakers, or "alewives," who brewed ale. Both married and unmarried women worked for a living. Because they were paid less than men, women often had two or more jobs.

Woolen "kirtle" fits close around the upper body

Leather purse serves as a pocket

Leather garters hold up stockings

Buckled leather shoes with thin soles

Wooden "pattens" worn over shoes when muddy

Woolen over-the-knee stockings

The great barons

EVERY NOBLEMAN was a vassal (p. 8) who had promised to serve his king. But many nobles grew so powerful that kings could not control them. By the 12th century, the strongest barons ruled what were really tiny, self-contained states with their own laws. The finery of their castle-courts often rivaled that of the king's, and many kept permanent armies at their beck and call. One French baron, the Sire de Coucy, had a bodyguard of 50 knights, each with ten followers. These small private armies sometimes rode out to plunder their neighbors in savage and pitiless raids. They posed a serious threat to the king if he did not keep his barons happy.

PARLIAMENTARY PIONEER
The English king usually governed through a Great Council of barons and churchmen. But Simon de Montfort (c. 1208–65) wanted to limit the powers of Henry III (1207–72). He led a rebellion in 1264, took the king prisoner, and summoned the first "parliament." This was made up of the old Council, plus two representatives from each county and town.

HIT MEN
Barons sometimes hired mercenary troops to do their fighting for them. These were bands of up to 3,000 soldiers of all nationalities – deserters from the Crusades, outlaws, and exiled knights.

VLAD DRACUL
Most infamous of all barons was the ghoulish Vlad Tepes of Romania (c. 1430–1476). According to legend, he put thousands of people to death by impaling them on stakes. He was nicknamed "Dracula," or "Dragon's son."

RALLY ROUND THE FLAG
Every nobleman had a banner such as this showing his own colors and emblems. Such flags were important rallying points for soldiers and knights on the battlefield.

THE BOAST OF HERALDRY
When knights rode into battle, their faces were hidden behind armor. So they identified themselves by carrying a coat of arms, or device, on their shield. By the 13th century, these devices were used not just by warriors, but by powerful baronial families.

Composite 15th-century flag

WARLORD
Charging full tilt at a band of helpless civilians, a fully armored knight, his face hidden behind a great helmet, was a chilling sight. Describing an attack by the men of a great baron on the town of Durham, England, in 1143, a monk recounted: "All that came in their way was destroyed; men were hung from the walls of their own houses; others they plunged into the bed of the river; everywhere throughout the town there were groans and all kinds of deaths."

14th-century visored "basinet"

THE GREAT CHARTER
In June 1215, the English barons forced King John (1167–1216) to sign the Magna Carta (Great Charter). This document limited the king's rights to tax the barons and to punish any man without a proper trial. But the Magna Carta did not recommend equal rights for all – ordinary people were scarcely mentioned. However, it was a crucial moment, the first time an English king had come under the control of the law.

King John's Great Seal

Wheel pommel

German battle ax, late 15th century

Italian war hammer, late 15th century

Single-handed French sword, 14th century

Fortified gatehouse

MORTAL COMBAT
The baron sat as judge in his own law court. If he could not reach a clear decision, he might allow a trial by combat. Accused and accuser would put on armor and fight each other with sword and ax – whoever won the battle, won the case. Most people preferred to hire champions to fight for them. But this was not a popular line of work. The loser might be suspected of surrendering on purpose, and have his hand chopped off as a punishment!

Double-edged blade with numerous battle scars

KEEP OUT!
Dotted around the medieval countryside, castles were impressive military strongholds. By the 12th century, many had massive towers of stone surrounded by high walls up to 33 ft (10 m) thick. They were so well fortified that an invading army could not capture them by a direct attack, but had to settle for a long siege. One of the most massive was at Carcassone in France (above), where the castle walls, with their 54 towers, enclosed the entire town.

The royal court

Love-heart decorated with tears

THE ROYAL COURT was the center and the showpiece of the kingdom. Here a monarch demonstrated his power with grand ceremonies and banquets, collected taxes, settled disputes, and made laws. It was particularly important to maintain control over the powerful barons. Henry II of England (1133–1189) held special court sessions to sort out arguments over land-holding, and Louis IX of France (1214–1270) insisted on listening to cases in person. Other monarchs amazed their subjects and visitors alike with the magnificence of their courts. Most astounding of all were the Sicilian castles of the Holy Roman Emperor (p. 8) Frederick II (1194–1250), which had golden floors, exotic animals, beautiful gardens, and dancing girls.

THE RIGHT TO RULE
Most medieval kings believed they had absolute power over their subjects, given to them by God. This sometimes led them to arrogant gestures – and disaster. Richard II of England (1367–1400) once sat for hours on his throne, glancing around. He merely wanted to watch his courtiers kneel when he looked at them. By 1399, Richard's despotic ways had made him so unpopular that he was deposed from his throne.

Lances measure about 13 ft (4 m)

LYRICS OF LOVE
Every court had its minstrels, who sang songs about love and brave deeds, accompanying themselves on the harp or the lute (p. 44). The greatest love songs were written by the troubadours, who flourished in southern France in the 12th century. Each troubadour wrote in praise of his idealized lady love.

LANCE A LOT
To rebel against the king was equivalent to defying God, but if a king was weak or poor, his powerful barons could be troublesome (pp. 24–25). Monarchs were eager to lure their noblemen to court, where they could keep an eye on them. One great attraction was the joust, a contest of fighting skills. Here, two armored knights canter toward each other, their lances held before them. The object was to hit your opponent on the head or chest and knock him off his horse.

Court ladies watch the tournament from the stand

Glittering shield may have been presented as a tournament prize

WAR GAMES
Pomp and ceremony were important parts of court life. The tourney, or mock battle, was a popular and spectacular way of amusing the court in the 11th century. While the king, queen, and courtiers looked on, large parties of knights charged at each other. If they were unhorsed, they went on fighting on foot. Tourneys were bloody and dangerous: during one fight at Cologne, more than 60 knights were killed.

"Tables" counter for playing a game similar to backgammon

IDLE PASTIMES
The lords and ladies of the court whiled away idle hours with indoor games such as backgammon, chess, and dice. Playing cards became popular in the 13th century.

OFFICIAL BUSINESS
The king made his wishes known through writs. His scribe's office produced hundreds of documents each year granting lands, and permission to raise armies, appoint officials, and order the payment of taxes. This writ, dated 1291, is a grant of game rights from Edward I of England (1239–1307) to one of his barons, Roger de Pilkington.

The royal seal makes the document official

A COURT OF LOVE
In the 12th century, courtly love became fashionable in royal circles. It was an artificial kind of passion, with strict rules. It had to be kept a secret, and the loved one had to be married – to someone else. Noble knights worshiped their ladies from afar, wrote long love poems, and vowed to do brave deeds for love. This parade shield shows a knight kneeling before his lady and bears the motto, "You, or Death."

15th-century Flemish shield

The medieval soldier

PEACE WAS RARE in medieval times, especially in Europe. The Crusades against the Muslim Turks lasted for three centuries, and the Hundred Years' War between England and France dragged on from 1337 to 1453. Even when there were no major campaigns, barons and brigands raided their neighbors. In the early Middle Ages, the armored knight ruled the battlefield. He scorned the foot soldiers, who were mostly a rabble of poor, terrified, and untrained peasants, pressed into battle by their lords. But by the 15th century, knights were fast going out of fashion and ordinary soldiers became much more important. Lords began employing professional warriors, who were well-paid, skilled, and used to obeying orders. Many worked as mercenary soldiers, hiring themselves out to the highest bidder.

THE CRUSADES
In 1095, the Pope called for a holy war against the Muslim Turks who controlled the Christian Holy Land of Palestine. A European army set off on the First Crusade and managed to recapture the holy city of Jerusalem, but the Turks soon advanced again. In all, there were eight crusades between 1147 and 1270, all of them failures. This 15th-century painting shows crusaders arriving at Damietta in Egypt.

ARCH ENEMY
Archers played a key role in the decline of the knight in the 15th century. Fired at the enemy from a safe distance, a deadly hail of arrows killed both men and horses. Without their horses, heavily armored knights were easy prey for foot soldiers.

"Glaive," a form of pole-weapon used for stabbing or knocking the enemy aside; it was safer to keep opponents at arm's length

Wooden drinking bowl for ale

Food bowl and spoon

Cloth-charcoal, or tinder / *Steel* / *Flint*

Flint, steel, and tinder for lighting campfires

Canvas kit bag

Chain splints keep swords from slicing through the arm

FOOTSORE AND HUNGRY
Life on the march could be very hard. A foot soldier would have to walk at least 6 miles (10 km) a day, and occasionally three times as far. His food bowl was often empty, and a large army soon consumed everything edible in the surrounding countryside. Starving French soldiers in the First Crusade of 1097 were told to feed on their enemies: "Are there not corpses of Turks in plenty? Cooked and salted they will be good to eat!"

Leather boots generally lasted about three months

Sheepskin mitten worn inside

Mitten gauntlet protects the hand and wrist

Visor limited vision, so it was lowered only during fierce fighting

Peak protects the neck

"Sallet" helmet

Military "bollock" dagger

Eating knife

HANDSOME RANSOM
A captured enemy could be a valuable acquisition. Important prisoners were often held to ransom for large sums of money. When King Richard I (1157–99) of England was captured in 1194, his country had to pay 150,000 marks – a huge sum in those days.

BELT-BAG
A soldier had to carry his personal belongings with him wherever he went, so luggage was kept to a minimum. Slung from his belt, this leather purse probably contained money, dice for gambling, needles and thread, and a kerchief.

HAND-TO-HAND FIGHTING
With a sword in his right hand and a buckler in his left, a soldier was a dangerous enemy. The buckler was not only used to deflect blows, but also to hit an opponent in the face, before jabbing or slashing with the sword. However, the soldier did most of his fighting with a glaive, and relied on his sword as a last resort. There were no rules of combat in medieval warfare, and most battles were terrifying free-for-alls.

Gauntlet limits wrist movement

Small fist-shield, or buckler, for punching

I'M ALL RIGHT, JACK
This military outfit would have been worn by a professional foot soldier in the late 15th century. Some of his gear would have been issued to him, and the rest was probably stolen or looted. Most soldiers at this time wore much less armor than the knights of old. A padded tunic, called a jack, with iron gauntlets and arm splints, gave good protection against sword cuts and even flying arrows.

Thin leather belt

Quilted "jack" made from multi-layered canvas

Close-fitting canvas doublet

Single-handed sword for hand-to-hand combat

29

The Church

THE CATHOLIC CHURCH was at the center of the medieval world. Unlike today, it was the only church in Europe, and all Christians belonged to it. With its own laws, lands, and taxes, the Church was a powerful institution. It governed almost every aspect of people's lives, from the practical to the spiritual. Most men and women, rich and poor, were baptized and married in church and attended mass every Sunday of their lives. When they died, their priest read them the last rites, and they were buried on church ground. For many, life on Earth was hard and short, but the Church said that if they followed the teachings of Christ, they would be rewarded in heaven. This idea gave the Church great power over people's hearts and minds.

LEADERS OF MEN
Archbishops were powerful men who sat on the king's council and played a leading role in government.

Censer is suspended on gilded chains

BIRD OF BLESSING
Suspended above the altar, this golden dove symbolized the Holy Spirit during the Eucharist – the Catholic ceremony where bread and wine are blessed and eaten to commemorate the sacrifice of Christ.

CHURCH TREASURES
By the 14th century, the Church had grown hugely wealthy. Money poured in from rents, tithes (p. 13), and the sale of indulgences (pardons for sins). Larger churches could afford to buy expensive sacramental vessels like this beautiful 14th-century silver chalice.

PARISH PRACTICES
The life of a parish priest was often a hard one. Many were poor men who lacked any serious education. Most of a priest's income came from fees charged for baptisms (above), marriages, and burial services. He also had his own land in the village, called the glebe, where he grew his own food. Apart from preaching, a village priest tended to the sick and poor, and the better-educated taught Latin and Bible stories to local boys.

Burning incense is placed inside the censer

SWINGING CENSERS
During mass, priests swung censers full of burning incense to purify the air. People believed that by attending mass regularly, they would be rewarded by God – and the more masses, the greater the reward. The wealthy could pay to have the "Trental," or 30 masses, said for them.

CONDEMNED TO THE FLAMES
Few people challenged the authority of the Church, but those who did were severely punished. People who disagreed with the Church's teachings were called heretics. They faced being brought to trial in a church court and, under its special laws, could be condemned to be whipped or burned at the stake. The Cathar sect of southern France rejected the beliefs of the Catholic Church with their claims that everything on Earth was created by the devil. In 1208, the Pope ordered a crusade against these heretics. Over the next 26 years, thousands of Cathars were tortured and burned in huge bonfires until they had been completely wiped out.

VISIONS OF HELL
The Church taught that when a person died, the good and bad deeds of their life were literally weighed in the balance by God. Their soul was either carried to heaven by angels or dragged off to hell by demons. Hell was a real and terrifying place for people in medieval times, and its torments were pictured in vivid detail in numerous paintings.

Carved wooden angels from a medieval church nave, or central hall

Angel swings a golden censer

Angel holds a tiny church

BISHOP'S MITER
Bishops were the local leaders of the Church. From their great cathedrals, they ruled over groups of parishes called dioceses. They usually came from noble families and were involved in affairs of state as well as those of the Church. Some were pious and learned men, but others were not – one 13th-century Italian bishop admitted that he did not believe in Christianity, and had only taken the office "because of its riches and honors."

14th-century bishop's miter, or hat

Picture shows the coronation of the Virgin by Christ

Angel holds a gilded casket

VICAR OF CHRIST
The Pope was head of the whole Church and represented God on Earth. This massive gilt ring belonged to Pope Eugenius IV, who ruled from 1431 to 1437.

Building a cathedral

IN THE EARLY MIDDLE AGES, large churches were built in the Roman style. They had massive pillars and thick walls to hold up the round-arched roofs. As a result, there were few windows, and Romanesque churches were sometimes dark and gloomy. By the 12th century, they were too small for the booming population of Europe, and for the growing stream of pilgrims (pp. 42–43). There was an explosion of cathedral building, starting in 1140 with the Abbey of St. Denis, near Paris. This was constructed in a startling new style, called Gothic, where the weight of the roof rested not on the walls, but on outside supports called buttresses. This allowed walls to be thinner, and pierced with tall windows that led the eye heavenward and flooded the cathedral with light.

SYMPHONIES IN STONE
Before 1350, 80 cathedrals were built in France alone. Among the first to use flying buttresses was Reims Cathedral, begun in 1211.

Shackle

Tapered slot stops the legs sliding out

The middle leg fits in last, wedging the other two firmly in place

Windlass

Heavy stone blocks raised in a basket

Mortar carrier

Mason preparing blocks

LIFTING WITH A LEWIS
Medieval stonemasons (pp. 52–53) used lifting devices called lewises to raise heavy stone blocks. The legs fit into a tapered slot cut into the top of the stone (shown in cross section above), and the lifting rope is hooked onto the shackle at the top. This small modern lewis can lift blocks weighing up to a ton.

MEN AT WORK
As the walls rose, masons had to work at greater heights. They stood on precarious wooden scaffolding lashed together with ropes. The stone was lifted up to them by a windlass, or hoist, attached to a big wheel turned by a man walking inside it. Working conditions were hazardous and there were many deaths.

Legs push outward as block is raised, so lewis does not fall out

Legs fit into a round hole

Centerings, or wooden frames, support the flying buttresses during construction; they are removed once the mortar has dried

Centerings are built at ground level, then hoisted into place

TIMELESS TOOLS
Lewises, like most other masonry tools (pp. 52–53), have changed little since medieval times. This kind of two-legged lewis was commonly used in the Middle Ages.

SOARING TO THE SKY

Gothic cathedrals were held up by skeletons of stone. The ribs were in the vaulted ceilings, which supported the massive stone-tiled roofs. These ribs of delicate stone rested on pillars and curved up to meet in a junction with a pointed arch. The vaults, or spaces, between the ribs were filled with a course of smaller stones. This method of building was so strong and light that cathedrals could be made higher than ever before. Throughout the 12th and 13th centuries, they soared up and up – the choir roof at Beauvais, France, reached a staggering 157 ft (48 m)!

LET THERE BE LIGHT

The tall, vertical lines of these late-14th-century windows draw the eye upward, which is why this High Gothic style is called "perpendicular." Delicately carved stone tracery (p. 53) supported vast panels of vivid stained glass (pp. 34–35).

FLYING FORCE

The other vital bones of a Gothic cathedral's skeleton were the buttresses. Stone roofs were so heavy that they pressed the ribbed vaults down onto the pillars and forced them outward. To counteract this, huge buttresses were built onto the outside, pushing inward. However, buttresses could not bear all the weight, especially at the top, where the ribs met the walls. Here, extra "flying" buttresses curved across the vault, transferring the outward thrust downward.

Space between blocks is filled with rubble

Gutter

Flying buttress reinforces the wall

Spout

EARLY EXAMPLE

The elaborate styles of High Gothic windows evolved from simple 13th-century lancets like these.

SPITTING IMAGES

Rainwater was drained off the roof into the gutters, and then shot out, well clear of the walls, through spouts. These spouts were often carved into gargoyles – grotesque faces that appeared to be spitting water.

The art of decoration

"I AM A POOR OLD WOMAN who knows nothing, who cannot read. But in the Church I see Paradise painted, and Hell where the damned broil." These were the words of a 15th-century French woman, and they spoke for millions of uneducated people in medieval Europe. For them, cathedrals and churches were not just places of worship, they were picture books and art galleries. The great cathedrals were filled with statues and carvings, painted panels and frescoes, which told stories of saints and biblical characters. Most wonderful of all were the stained glass windows through which light streamed in dazzling, brilliant colors.

ICONS FROM THE EAST
The inspiration for Europe's church decorators came from the glittering Eastern city of Byzantium (modern-day Istanbul). This sacred picture, or icon, of Christ glows with gold and rich colors. Icons were worshiped as holy objects.

Hog's-hair scrub

Stippler for scraping away highlights once a color wash has been applied

Tracing brush for applying fine lines

Latherkin for smoothing out the lead

Groziers for snipping bits off a glass shape; flint was used in medieval times

Modern glaziers' tools

Line of sketch, or cartoon

Soldered joint

THE WHOLE PICTURE
Like a fragile and beautiful jigsaw puzzle, the stained glass pieces are fitted together with the lead. The glass slides into grooves in each side of the lead strips, and the whole assembly is held firm with large horseshoe nails. Finally, the joints between the strips are soldered, and putty is applied to seal in glass. The completed panel is then set with others into the delicate stone tracery (p. 53) of a window. The lead will last for over 100 years before it needs replacing.

GLAZIERS AND GROZIERS
Most glass came to the glass painters, or glaziers, from countryside kilns. It was already colored, and the glaziers cut and shaped the glass pieces. They could vary the colors by scraping away the surface or painting it.

Wicked devil urges on the three gossips

Line of clear glass was known as the white, or sacrificial, line, because it was most likely to be broken when the panel was removed for re-leading

Cut and painted glass shape

STORIES IN GLASS
Stained glass windows were like cartoon strips. Through pictures, they taught religious lessons and the stories of the Bible to those who could not read. This panel depicts three gossiping women with leering devils at their shoulders. The moral is clear – don't speak badly of your neighbors!

CUT AND COLORED
In medieval times, the design for a window was drawn onto a board coated with chalk and water. Glass pieces were placed over the design and cut to shape, using a hot iron to score the glass. Final trimming was done by nibbling the edges with a grozier. The details of the picture were painted on with enamel, and the glass was fired to fuse in the paint.

Space left for lead is called the "cut line"

The lead has grooves along each side into which the glass fits

Charlemagne (p. 6) was a renowned Christian king

BEAUTIFUL BLUE
Medieval glassmakers produced colors by adding metallic oxides to the molten glass. The glowing colors they created were named after precious stones – ruby red, emerald green, and sapphire blue. The recipes for different colors were closely guarded secrets and most have since been lost. The beautiful blue glass in these famous windows at Chartres Cathedral, France, was known as *bleu de ciel* – "heavenly blue."

Large nails hold the jigsaw of glass and lead together before soldering

Lead is soft and can be shaped around the glass quite easily

A SHINING EXAMPLE
Altarpieces usually portrayed great moments from the story of Christ. This altar panel was painted in 1333 for Siena Cathedral, Italy, by Simone Martini and Lippo Memmi. It shows the Archangel Gabriel announcing to Mary that she will bear the baby Jesus. The style is much more natural than the stiff and formal design of Byzantine icons. The central figures, glowing against a golden background, are full of graceful movement.

An altarpiece is set behind the altar

Holy orders

"WE MUST FORM A SCHOOL IN THE LORD'S SERVICE," wrote St. Benedict in the sixth century. He founded a monastery at Monte Cassino in Italy where monks could live, work, and pray together. The monks became known as the Benedictines because they followed St. Benedict's "Rule," which instructed them to make three vows – of poverty (to own no property), chastity (never to marry), and obedience (to obey the orders of their leaders). Making these vows was a serious undertaking, so St. Benedict ordered that every novice, or newcomer, should live in the monastery for a year before committing himself. Once he had made his vows, a novice had the crown of his head shaved in a tonsure and became a brother of the order. In time, monasteries and convents throughout Europe adopted St. Benedict's Rule.

12th-century Celtic monk

Tonsure

Bone stylus

Wax tablet on a horn base

WAX COPY BOOK
Monks spent a lot of time copying out prayers and psalms by hand. They often wrote on wax tablets with a stylus, or scratcher. Copying holy passages was also a way of serving God. St. Bernard (1090–1153) told monks, "Every word you write is a blow that smites the devil."

THE HISTORY MAN
Many monks were well educated, and monasteries became centers of learning. St. Bede (c. 673–735), also known as the Venerable Bede, was an English Benedictine monk who devoted his life to writing and scholarship. He wrote books on science, religion, and history, including the great *Ecclesiastical History of the English Nation*. Without monks like Bede, we would know much less about the history of the Middle Ages.

NO LIGHT IN THE DARKNESS
St. Benedict's Rule allowed for basic comforts, but life in a monastery was never easy. At first, monks were not allowed candles for reading at services – they had to learn all the prayers, psalms, and other forms of worship by heart.

OUT OF ORDER
By the tenth century, many religious houses had become too relaxed. The monk below has been placed in the stocks with his mistress as a punishment for an illicit affair. Some French monks thought that the ideals of St. Benedict were being forgotten and formed a new order at Cluny in 910. The Cluniacs tried to follow the strict and simple rules laid down by St. Benedict. Other new orders were the Carthusians, who believed in a life of silent prayer, and the Cistercians, who thought that hard work was the best way to serve God.

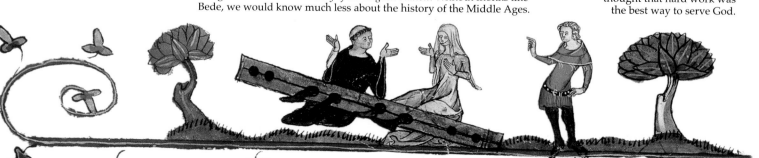

THE FRANCISCANS

St. Francis of Assisi (c. 1182–1226) was the son of a rich man, yet he gave away all his possessions to live like one of Christ's disciples. He founded a new order of holy brothers in Italy called Franciscan friars. Instead of living in monasteries, they took the word of God to the people, traveling about preaching and begging for their food. An order of Franciscan nuns was founded by St. Clare, one of St. Francis's followers.

Plain rope belt

Bare feet

HEAD WARMER

In winter, chilly drafts whistled through the stone corridors and bare cells of a monastery. Only the sickroom was always heated. Although the monastic way of life was often harsh, St. Benedict did not believe that monks should sacrifice their health in the service of God. His Rule stated that a monk's clothes should be plain but comfortable, and Benedictines were allowed to wear linen coifs such as this one to keep their heads warm. The Cistercians rejected such soft ways. Many of them went barefoot, and some even wore hairy underclothes as a sign of their devotion to God.

Linen shift worn underneath the habit

Paternoster, or wooden bead rosary, for counting prayers

Eating knife

Warm cloak worn in cold weather

Benedictines were allowed to wear leather belts

Long woolen habit was supposed to emulate Roman clothing

Simple, hand-sewn leather shoes; Benedictines did not have to wear sandals

HABIT OF A LIFETIME

The oldest and largest of the monastic orders, the Benedictines were known as the Black Monks because of the color of their habits. Each of the new orders formed in the 10th, 11th, and 12th centuries had its own distinguishing dress. For example, the Cistercians wore rough tunics of undyed wool and became known as the White Monks. Nevertheless, the basic style of the habit has remained the same to this day.

Life in a monastery

MONASTERIES AND CONVENTS were worlds of their own. Ruled by an abbot or an abbess, they were cut off from society and governed by special rules. When a novice (p. 36) entered a holy order, he or she was expected to stay there for the rest of his or her life. From that moment on, every part of his or her day was accounted for. Much of the time was spent attending the eight daily church services and reading or copying religious texts. Other duties included caring for the poor and sick, teaching younger members of the order, or tending to the gardens, fishponds, mill, and farm. There was a general rule of silence in most religious houses, and daily tasks had to be carried out without speaking. Although they lived apart from society, monks and nuns served an important role in the community. They provided food for the poor, care for the sick, and accommodation for pilgrims and other travelers.

ROUND OF PRAYERS
Monks went to the monastery church eight times a day in an unchanging round of offices, or services. The first, Matins, began at two o'clock in the morning, and dormitories were built near the church so that the monks wouldn't be late for services. In the early 11th century, monks at Canterbury, England, had to sing 55 psalms, one after the other, without sitting down. The Benedictines shown here at least have pews to rest on.

Single-chambered wicker beehive daubed with clay

Straw "hackle," or jacket, placed over the hive in winter to keep the bees warm

Statue of Mary and Jesus

Wicker beehive made from woven willow or hazel

Abbey church

BUSY BEES
The Cistercians (p. 36) believed that performing hard manual labor was the best way to lead a holy life. They built large monasteries in remote rural areas where they could farm the land in peace. Their estates grew so big that lay brothers (those who had taken holy vows but lacked the education to become monks) were taken on to help. Most monasteries had to produce their own food. These skeps, or beehives, provided honey to eat and wax for candles.

CARE IN A CONVENT
Nuns took the same vows as monks (p. 36) and lived in much the same way. Devoted to serving the poor, most convents and monasteries ran hospitals to care for the sick. These were open to all, and nuns and monks were instructed to "receive the patients as you would Christ Himself." The medicines and treatments may have been primitive (pp. 60–61), but at least patients were given food and a clean bed. Without the work of the Church, there would have been very little health care in the Middle Ages.

Model of an abbey in the 15th century

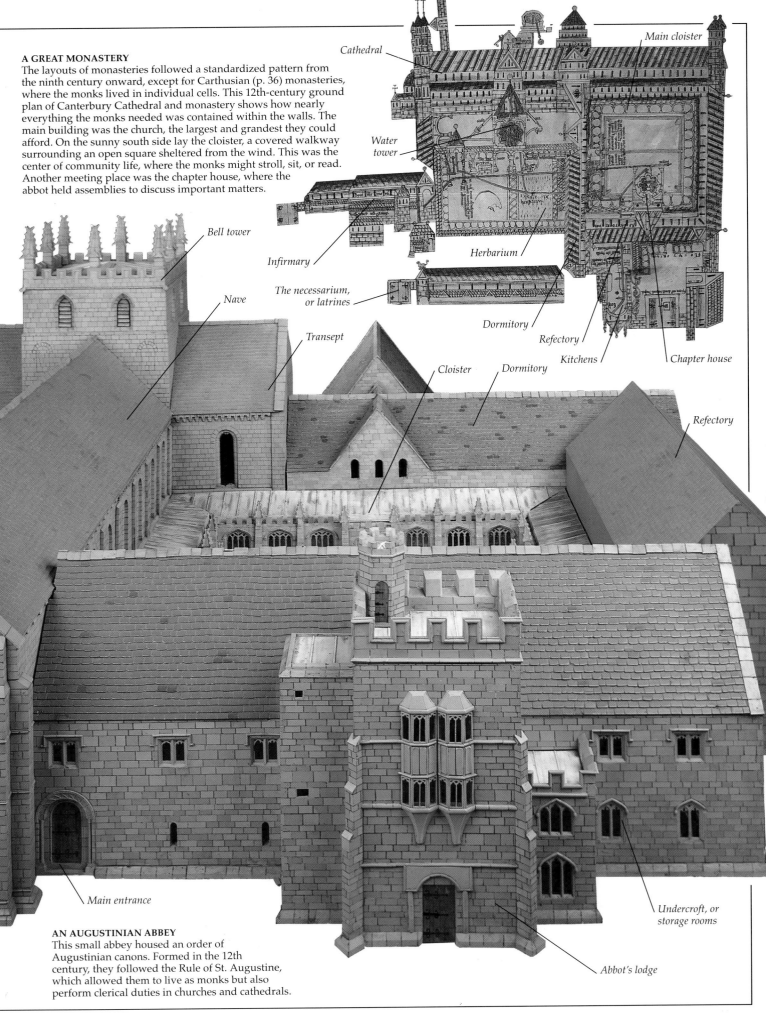

A GREAT MONASTERY

The layouts of monasteries followed a standardized pattern from the ninth century onward, except for Carthusian (p. 36) monasteries, where the monks lived in individual cells. This 12th-century ground plan of Canterbury Cathedral and monastery shows how nearly everything the monks needed was contained within the walls. The main building was the church, the largest and grandest they could afford. On the sunny south side lay the cloister, a covered walkway surrounding an open square sheltered from the wind. This was the center of community life, where the monks might stroll, sit, or read. Another meeting place was the chapter house, where the abbot held assemblies to discuss important matters.

Cathedral

Main cloister

Water tower

Herbarium

Infirmary

The necessarium, or latrines

Dormitory

Refectory

Kitchens

Chapter house

Bell tower

Nave

Transept

Cloister

Dormitory

Refectory

Main entrance

Undercroft, or storage rooms

Abbot's lodge

AN AUGUSTINIAN ABBEY

This small abbey housed an order of Augustinian canons. Formed in the 12th century, they followed the Rule of St. Augustine, which allowed them to live as monks but also perform clerical duties in churches and cathedrals.

The written word

UNTIL 1100, BOOKS WERE RARE and were usually found only in monastery libraries. Everything was written by hand, and monks spent many hours in the "scriptorium," copying out religious texts. A long manuscript such as the Bible might take one scribe a year to complete. As a way of glorifying God, many manuscripts were beautifully illuminated, or decorated, with jewel-like paints and precious gold leaf. After 1200, books became more common, especially when the first universities opened in Paris and Bologna. Professional scribes and illuminators began to produce books as well as the monks, often making copies to order for wealthy customers. Personal books of psalms, called psalters, became popular among the aristocracy.

1 GESSO WORK
One of the most striking features of medieval manuscripts are the beautifully decorated capital letters that begin each page. Painted in vibrant colors, they were often gilded with gold leaf to make them even brighter. The first stage of illuminating a letter is applying the gesso, a kind of glue made from plaster, white lead, water, sugar, and eggwhite, which makes a sticky surface for the gold leaf.

The gold leaf only sticks to the moist gesso

The molded gesso gives a 3-D effect to the gilded leaves

Each leaf is burnished separately

3 BURNISHED BRIGHT
Once the gold leaf has set into the gesso, the illuminator rubs it, or burnishes it, to make it shiny. The traditional burnishing tool was a dog's or wolf's tooth attached to a wooden handle. Finally, the rest of the background is carefully painted in around the gilding.

2 GILDING THE LETTER
The gesso is left to set over night, and the next day the illuminator smooths any rough edges and breathes on the gesso to make it slightly moist. He then lays a sheet of gold leaf over the gesso, covers it with a silk cloth, and presses it firmly onto the glue. The surplus gold is removed with a soft brush.

SCRIBES AND SCHOLARS
However hard scribes worked, books remained scarce. Few people could afford to buy them, and scholars had to travel to monastic libraries to study the texts they wanted. This statue of a scholar is from Chartres Cathedral, France.

4 SHINING THROUGH THE AGES
The finished letter is like a tiny work of art. Apart from leaves and flowers, many illuminated initials contain pictures of people and animals. If the gold is properly burnished, it will never fade – most medieval manuscripts still shine brightly today.

Curling leaves are a popular "Gothic" design

Bone eyeglasses

SIGHT FOR SORE EYES
Hours of close copying often damaged the eyesight. Europeans first started wearing eyeglasses in the 13th century. The invention of printing in the 1450s (p. 62) made more books available, and the sale of glasses rocketed.

The paternoster, or Lord's prayer, written in Latin

Feather is rarely left on the quill because it gets in the way

Inkwell slots into a hole in the desk

Pater noster qui es in caelis · Sanctificetur nomen tuum · Adveniat regnum tuum · Fiat voluntas tua sicut in caelo et in tem · Panem nostrum quotidianum da nobis hodie · Et dimitte nobis debita nostra sicut et nos dimittimus debitoribus nostris · Et ne nos inducas in temptatione · Sed libera nos a malo · Amen ·

Horn "book" hangs from a belt

Point used for pricking outlines on parchment

Stylus   Goose quills   Horn inkwells

A LITTLE LEARNING
Most schooling in the Middle Ages took place in monasteries, convents, and cathedrals. Children (mostly boys who were destined for holy orders) received a basic education in reading and writing, and spent much of their time learning prayers and Bible passages by heart – all in Latin. They were often forbidden to talk or play, and were beaten with a birch rod when their attention wandered!

FIRST LESSONS
Children began learning to read with a horn book such as this, first used in the 1450s. The alphabet or prayer was covered with a transparent sheet of horn to protect it from grubby fingers.

Selection of quills

Jug of ale or weak wine for refreshment

Sloping desk

Straight-backed chair made from white ash wood

Drinking vessel

Horn books to copy from

Tabletop folds backward

SEAT FOR A SCRIBE
A scribe might sit for hours at his work copying out Latin texts in beautiful, well-formed script. He rested his parchment on a sloping desk, which made it easier to hold his pen at right angles (quills wrote best this way). In his left hand, he held a penknife, which he used to hold down the page, to scrape out mistakes, and to sharpen his quill – often up to 60 times a day.

Cushion made long hours of work more comfortable

Tabula plicata, *or folding table, can be stored flat against a wall*

Decoration carved only on the side that faces the room

"Turned" chair-leg, decorated with bands of vermilion paint

Saints and pilgrims

Most people in the Middle Ages hoped to go on a pilgrimage to a holy shrine at some point in their lives. They went for many reasons – as proof of their devotion to God, as an act of penance for their sins, or to find a cure for an illness. The holy city of Jerusalem was a favorite destination, as were Rome, where both St. Peter and St. Paul were believed to be buried, the shrine of St. James at Santiago de Compostela in Spain, and Canterbury Cathedral in England. On the road, rich and poor traveled together, and for many, pilgrimages were a sort of holiday. To pass the time, people sang songs and hymns, played pipes, and told stories over their evening meals in roadside taverns.

ON THE ROAD
In the early Middle Ages, most pilgrims traveled on foot. They wore long woolen tunics called sclaveins, broad-brimmed felt hats, and sandals.

Front part of reliquary contains a holy cross set in pearls and rock crystal

Tiny flask, or ampulla, for holy water

Scallop-shell emblem of Santiago de Compostela

Pewter badge of St. Thomas Becket

PORTABLE RELICS
Holy relics, or the bones of saints, were not only kept in shrines. People carried them in bags around their necks or in beautifully decorated cases like this one. Knights often had relics placed in their sword hilts.

SIGN OF THE SHRINE
Like modern tourists, medieval pilgrims often sported badges to show that they had been to a certain shrine. They wore them on their hats to make it clear that they were on a holy journey and had the right to protection. The scallop shell was a popular emblem.

Back part of reliquary contains pieces of bone, or relics, set in gold as a sign of their value

Figure of Christ

Becket's body is laid in a shroud

Becket is carried to Heaven by angels

A MARTYR'S BONES
This 12th-century reliquary casket depicts the murder of Archbishop Thomas Becket (on Henry II's orders) in Canterbury Cathedral in 1170. Becket became a saint, and Canterbury, resting place of his bones, quickly became a place of pilgrimage.

One of the King's knights slices off Becket's head

THE PILGRIM'S POET
Geoffrey Chaucer (c. 1340–1400) wrote the best-loved book about pilgrims, *The Canterbury Tales*. It is a series of stories in verse told by a party of 30 pilgrims to pass the time as they ride to Canterbury. The pilgrims, who include a knight, a miller, a friar, a prioress, and a cook, portray a vivid and often hilarious picture of medieval life.

Crown of semi-precious stones

INSIDE STORY
This wooden head fits inside the large gold head and was the real receptacle for the relics of St. Eustace.

Wealthy pilgrims on horseback

PILGRIM'S PROGRESS
Robbers and brigands were a constant threat to the medieval traveler, so pilgrims journeyed together in groups for safety, sometimes even taking an armed escort. On popular routes, such as the one to Santiago de Compostela in Spain, local rulers built special roads and bridges, and monks set up hostels, spaced a day's journey apart.

Head is made of silver gilded with gold

HOLY HEAD
A reliquary was a special casket for holding relics, such as the bones of a saint or a splinter of Christ's cross. Relics were displayed in shrines, where they were visited by pilgrims. People believed they had almost magical powers, such as the power to cure diseases or bring victory in battle. This beautiful 13th-century gilded head contained the relics of St. Eustace, an early Christian saint, and was displayed in Basel Cathedral, Switzerland.

The Islamic world

THE PROPHET MUHAMMAD, founder of Islam, died in 632. Within 100 years, Arab armies had conquered a vast empire that stretched from Spain and North Africa to Persia and India. International trade flourished in the Islamic world, spreading ideas as well as goods. Muslim scientists became particularly advanced in the fields of medicine and mathematics: they were skilled surgeons and eye doctors, invented algebra (from the Arabic *al-jebr*), and introduced the Arabic numeral system to Europe, a version of which is still in use today. Although the Christians saw the Muslims as an "infidel" race and an almost inhuman enemy during the Crusades, they learned much from this highly advanced civilization as trade links grew stronger.

GLITTERING PRIZE
The rich cities of the Islamic world were prime targets for the plundering crusaders (p. 28). In 1099, they succeeded in overrunning the holy city of Jerusalem, killing its inhabitants, and pillaging its vast treasures.

Inlaid decoration

Traditional Arabic pattern

MUSLIM MARVELS
The lute was one of the symbols of medieval European music, but its true origin was in the Islamic world, where it was known as *al-'ud*. Many Muslim caliphs, or rulers, were great patrons of art and learning, and fostered the work of musicians, poets, artists, and scholars at their courts. The lute was just one of many inventions and ideas that came to Europe from the Muslim empire.

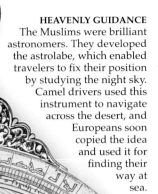

HEAVENLY GUIDANCE
The Muslims were brilliant astronomers. They developed the astrolabe, which enabled travelers to fix their position by studying the night sky. Camel drivers used this instrument to navigate across the desert, and Europeans soon copied the idea and used it for finding their way at sea.

LUXURY TRAIN
Camel trains carried a huge range of goods across the deserts and mountains of the Islamic world. In the dazzling bazaars of Baghdad and Damascus, the wealthy could buy a stunning variety of luxury goods, from Persian carpets and African ivory, to Asian silks, spices, jewels, and furs.

HERO OF A HOLY WAR
Saladin (1137–1193) was a great Islamic sultan who led the Muslim armies against the crusaders, and recaptured Jerusalem. He was respected even by his enemies as a brilliant general and a wise man.

MEDICINE MEN
Even as the Crusades were raging, Europeans learned a great deal from Islamic doctors, whose knowledge was far in advance of their own. Cures for numerous ills could be bought in apothecaries such as this. In the 11th century, the great Arab doctor Avicenna (980–1037) wrote a medical encyclopedia that became the single greatest influence on medieval medicine.

ARTS AND CRAFTS
Islamic craftsmen were renowned for their beautiful enamel work. They usually decorated religious artifacts, such as this 13th-century mosque lamp, with Arabic words and geometric patterns, because Islamic tradition banned images of human figures and other living things from religious buildings.

Trade and commerce

THE EARLIEST MEDIEVAL MERCHANTS were peddlers, who sold goods to villages and towns. By the 12th century, Europe had grown more prosperous and more goods were produced. Merchants were no longer simply wandering adventurers. They became dealers, employers, and ship owners, sending their carriers along a network of trade routes linking the European cities. By 1300, cargo ships from Genoa and Venice were taking precious metals, silks, and other luxuries from the eastern Mediterranean out to England and Flanders (Belgium). There they picked up wool, coal, and timber for the return voyage. German and Dutch ships took iron, copper, and lead south to the Mediterranean, and brought back wine, oil, and salt.

Quills were trimmed before use

One half of a tally stick

TALLY STICK
A debt could be recorded on a tally stick. Notches were cut into it to record the amount, then the stick was split in two and each party kept half. When the debt was settled, the tally was destroyed or kept as a record.

CANDLE WAX
This tiny candle was used to melt the wax for sealing letters and documents.

BALANCING THE BOOKS
Merchants needed to keep careful accounts of their money. Traders in 14th-century Florence developed a system of double-entry bookkeeping. Each deal was recorded in two ledgers – one for credits, the other for debits. The amounts in each ledger should always balance.

Horn inkwell and quill

KEEP THE CHANGE
Merchants kept small numbers of coins in money boxes like this. Most coins were silver, but in 1252, the city of Florence minted the first gold coin since Roman times – the golden florin.

14th-century document seal

SIGNED AND SEALED
As trading methods grew more complex, much more paperwork was needed. Merchants had to employ clerks and scribes to help them. There were letters giving details of business deals, bills of sale, orders, contracts to suppliers, and documents promising payment. All of these had to be signed and marked with the wax seals of the merchants involved.

Late-medieval
purse frame

A WOODEN CALCULATOR
For most of the Middle Ages, paper was
scarce and few people could read or
write, so traders added up their cash
on a counter board marked into
columns. Jettons, or counters,
were added to a column until
they reached a certain total
(usually ten). Then they
were removed, and
counting began in
the next column.

THE HANSEATIC LEAGUE
In the 13th century, trading towns on the
North Sea and Baltic coasts, including
Hamburg (above), united to form the
Hanseatic League. Their aim was to
help each other in fighting pirates
and bandits and to gain exclusive
control of foreign trade.
The league grew very
powerful – by 1400
it had offices in
160 towns in
northern
Europe.

Silver deniers and purse

WEIGHING IT UP
Most medieval
merchants carried
small coin balances for
weighing different currencies
to determine their value.

Tumbrel coin
balance

*Spike sticks
into desktop*

14th-century
keys for locking
away valuables

MONEY MEN
Banking began
in Italy with
moneylenders who
did business on benches,
or banks. They grew rich
on the interest they charged
for their services. The cities of
Florence, Venice, Siena, and Genoa
became particularly prosperous.
However, the business was not without its
hazards – two wealthy banks in Florence were
ruined in the 1350s when Edward III of England
(1327–77) was unable to repay a massive loan.

Life in the town

As TRADE GREW, so did towns. At first they were part of a lord's or king's domain, but as townsmen became wealthier they resented having to work for someone else. In northern France there were violent scenes as towns struggled to become independent "communes." In England the process was more peaceful. Town dwellers agreed to pay a fixed sum each year in return for a royal charter, which granted them the right to govern themselves. The town then became a free "borough" with the power to make its own laws, form trade guilds (p. 50), and raise taxes. The people also became "burgesses," or free citizens.

THE NIGHT WATCH
At sunset, the town bells rang to sound the curfew. This meant that everyone had to finish work and go home. There were no streetlights in medieval towns, and the streets could be dangerous places after dark. Night watchmen patrolled with lanterns to deter criminals.

STREET SIGNS
Towns were first and foremost centers of trade with bustling streets full of shops. Since few people could read, many shops advertised their wares by hanging out a symbol of their trade, such as a loaf for a baker or a basin for a barber (seen in the middle of the picture). In some towns, traders or craftsmen of the same type had shops in the same street, so shoemakers worked in Shoe Lane, tailors on Threadneedle Street, fishmongers in the Rue de la Poissonerie, and so on.

15th-century French city

WALLED IN
Medieval towns were surrounded by stone walls. These were not only to keep out rogues and criminals. They also made sure that merchants and other visitors could enter only by the gates, where they had to pay a toll. Town gates were opened at dawn and locked at dusk.

THE LORD MAYOR
Most towns were governed by an elected mayor and a local council. Mayors became powerful figures who were often courted by lords and kings. Some even loaned money to the monarch. Dick Whittington (c. 1358–1423) was a famous English mayor. The son of a knight, he became a wealthy merchant and was elected Lord Mayor of London three times.

TOWERS THAT BE
Powerful families struggled to gain control of the new communes and boroughs. In Italy, they built defensive towers as symbols of their wealth and importance. At San Gimignano in Tuscany, over 70 towers were erected in the 12th century. Eventually, most town councils forbade any building higher than the town hall.

GARDEY LOO!
Slop pails and chamber pots were emptied out of windows with the cry "Gardey loo!", from the French *"gardez l'eau"*, meaning "Look out, water!" Town dwellers were naturally wary when walking down the street!

"Half-moon" leather knife

Spike possibly used to make holes for stitching

Hook-like leather knife

Upper stories were home to the shopkeeper's family

A staircase at the rear leads to the upper chambers

LIVING OVER THE SHOP
Most craftsmen had their workshops on the ground floors of their homes. These also served as shops, and finished goods were displayed on a hinged shelf at the front. In the evening, shutters were pulled down for security. The shopkeeper usually had a storeroom at the back, and he and his family lived on the floors above. This 15th-century building is divided into two shops. Only the smaller shop on the right has access to the upper floors, which means that the other was probably rented out to another business.

Sole made from tough cattle hide

Waxed linen thread

Upper made from goatskin, which is strong and flexible

LEAN STREETS
There was a limited amount of space within the walls of a medieval town, and houses were built very close together. To maximize space, the upper stories of buildings were "jettied," or built jutting out above the ground floors. In some places, the houses on either side almost touched each other, making the streets gloomy and airless.

Half-finished shoe will be turned other way out when complete

TOWN TRADE
Craftsmen such as shoemakers worked at windows that opened onto the street, giving them the opportunity to show off their skills to passersby. Medieval shoemakers were known as cordwainers, after the best shoe leather from Córdoba in Spain. These long-toed "poulaine" shoes were fashionable in the late 14th century and would have been sold to a wealthy merchant or burgess.

Emblem of the Armorers' Guild

The guild masters

I<small>N</small> 1262, A BOOK OF TRADES compiled in Paris listed over 100 different crafts, each of which had its own guild, or association. By the 1420s, guilds existed in most big towns throughout Europe and their numbers were still growing. A guild's main objective was to gain high wages and exclusive control of their business for their members. They fixed prices and standards of work and made sure that no outsiders competed with them. Guilds also supported members who fell on hard times, providing them with money from a central fund. In time, the guilds grew rich and powerful. They built grand guildhalls, paraded in fine costume on special occasions, and often played an important role in civic affairs.

THE ARMORERS
The Armorers' Guild maintained the standards of the craftsmen who made plate armor. Near Milan in Italy, one of the centers of armor-making in the 15th century, whole villages were employed in the trade.

WOMEN AT WORK
Most guilds would not allow women members, but this did not prevent women from learning skilled trades. Many worked with their husbands or fathers. Silk-weaving in London was almost entirely done by women, although they were not allowed to form their own guild.

Mail coif

Coiled wire

Flap protects the mouth

Rings snipped off wire

Rivets

Each ring end is flattened and linked by a rivet

ANOTHER FINE MESH
Mail-making was a skilled and painstaking process. Each ring was linked to four others and held together by a tiny rivet. An entire suit of mail could be made up of thousands of rings.

Pliers

Green comes from woad leaves and weld

Blue produced by woad or indigo dyes

Linen dyed with madder root

Bright orange and red dyes come from madder roots

Oak bark gives a brown color

Yellow comes from dyers' green weed, or weld

Plant-dyed wools

Emblem of the Ropemakers' Guild

MASTER DYERS
In the Middle Ages, cloth-making was a gigantic industry that employed a large array of guild crafts. There were the weavers, the fullers and walkers (who cleaned and compacted the cloth), the carders (who brushed it), and the shearmen (who trimmed it). Then there were the dyers, who dyed the cloth in huge heated vats full of dye.

GUILDHALLS

The richer guilds had chambers or guildhalls, which proudly displayed their coats of arms. Here members met for a banquet on the anniversary of their patron saint, and the guild court sat to settle disputes and punish members who had disobeyed the strict rules.

"Borrelais" hat derived from a hood worn the wrong way around

Emblem of the Bakers' Guild

THE GUILD MASTER

This fine costume would have been worn by a middle-class merchant or business owner in the 1400s. Toward the end of the Middle Ages, the wealthier merchants began to control the guilds' affairs for their own ends. They bought the raw materials and sold the finished goods, and were more interested in making money than in the welfare of the poorer tradesmen. Guild masters also became important civic figures who often had the final say in the election of the town mayor.

Fashionable fur-trimmed sleeves

Decorated leather purse

Personal eating knife

Blue woolen doublet lined with linen

LEARNING A TRADE

Getting to the top of a guild was a long and hard process. An apprentice had to pay a large sum of money just to start. His apprenticeship lasted for about seven years, during which he learned every aspect of the craft from a master (here seen judging work by a mason and a carpenter). After this, he became a journeyman (from the French *journée* or "day") and worked for a daily wage. A journeyman could one day become a master – as long as he paid the right fees.

Fine woolen coat made with a large amount of material as a sign of wealth

The codpiece, which served as a fly, became fashionable after 1450

Expensive mid-calf leather boots

"Joined" hose were made to measure

Emblem of the Shoemakers' Guild

The stonemasons

OF ALL MEDIEVAL CRAFTSMEN, skilled masons were the most highly paid and respected. It was they who built the great cathedrals and castles that still rise above many European towns and cities. Before they formed exclusive guilds (pp. 50–51) in the 14th century, masons organized their trade from their lodges. These were the masons' headquarters on the building site where they worked in bad weather, ate their meals, and discussed trade secrets. Rules and working conditions were set out by the lodge leaders. Masons learned their craft on the site itself, often serving an apprenticeship of up to seven years. The most talented might go on to become master masons, with the responsibility for designing and overseeing the building of an entire cathedral.

"Stock" rests on top of the stone

Blade measures depth

SINKING SQUARE
Each stone had to be worked precisely to shape before being hoisted into position. The sinking square was used to measure the depth of holes or grooves and to check that the corners were square.

SCORING A CURVE
The mason had to mark out his stone to show him where to cut or carve. To mark a curved line parallel to the edge, he used a box trammel. Holding the wooden handle firmly against the edge, he dragged it along. The trammel point moved across the stone, scoring a line.

Sharp point scores the stone

SQUARED UP
The square was one of the mason's most important tools. It was used for making sure corners were straight.

Pitching tool for making clean breaks in rough stone

Well-worn chisel-head

PITCHER THIS
Every single stone in a cathedral would have taken about a day to cut and finish. Because it was heavy and expensive to transport, the stone was cut approximately to size at the quarry. At the building site, the mason's first job was to finish cutting the rough stone with a big curved saw. Then he used a hammer, a heavy, blunt chisel called a pitching tool, and a punch (right) to chip off the larger lumps and produce nearly straight edges.

Hammer-headed chisels

Punch for chipping off large bits of stone

HEAVY LUMP
The lump hammer was used for hitting hammer-headed chisels in the rough shaping work.

UNITED BY DIVIDERS
Dividers, or wing compasses, became the mason's special emblem. They were used mainly to measure a distance on a template, and then transfer the measurement to a piece of stone.

Medieval dividers

Modern masons mark out a block with pencil lines

Template for the cross-section of the joint

Paper template for a piece of window tracery

Joint

ACCORDING TO PLAN
The template, or pattern, for each stone was cut out of board, leather, or parchment and laid over the stone for the mason to copy.

MARKING OUT
The mason selected a block of stone that had been trimmed square and smooth on which to mark out the template. He then scribed, or scratched, around the edges.

Drafting chisel for carving the first outline

Gouge for working curved surfaces

Claw chisel for scraping away stone

Mallet-headed chisels for use with a mallet

CHOOSING A CHISEL
An apprentice mason had to learn to handle a bewildering array of chisels. Each mason owned his own tools, all of which bore his personal mark. They were usually passed down from generation to generation. The design of modern masonry tools like these has changed little since medieval times.

Stone relief (left) dedicated to the Stonemasons' Guild from the church of Or San Michele in Florence

WORKS OF ART
Some stonemasons became specialist sculptors. Intricate carvings such as the figures, foliage, and animals that decorated the great cathedrals were created by highly skilled "imaginators."

MASTER MIND
The master mason was in charge of everything on the building site, from designing the building to hiring workers and ordering stone from the quarry. His job was that of an architect and a foreman all rolled into one – he set out plans and templates for his workers, but was also expected to work alongside them on occasion.

Cusp (from the Latin cuspis *which means "spearhead")*

MASONS' MARK
A mason "signed" each finished stone with his personal mark to show how much work he had completed.

THE FINISHED ARTICLE
The carving of ornamental stonework, such as the stone ribs, or tracery, that supported stained glass windows, took many years to master. Experienced stonemasons could carve any number of complex pieces. This section of tracery links the delicate ribs in the upper part of a window.

SHAPING THE STONE
The final shaping of the stone was the job of a banker mason who worked on a bank, or bench. Using chisels, gouges, and saws, he cut the stone to the scribed pattern.

Masons rub away tool marks on soft stone with a toothed iron plate called a cock's comb, or drag

WORKING IN THE LODGE
Outside building work was only done in the good weather of the summer months. In winter, stonemasons labored on under cover in their lodge, designing, marking out, and cutting pieces of stone.

Fairs and feast days

BOTH PEASANTS AND TOWN-DWELLERS looked forward to the festivals and fairs that marked the important days of the year. On "holy days," or holidays, such as Christmas and Easter, everyone took time off work to attend special church services, banquets, and festivities. Great trade fairs, often held on the feast days of saints, were also occasions for fun. Merchants came from all over Europe to buy and sell their goods and were entertained by musicians, acrobats, and players. Other special events that were related to different times of the year were May Day, Midsummer's Eve, and the Harvest Home.

NO DICE
Although it was frowned upon by the Church, gambling was one of the most widespread of medieval pastimes. People played dice games and betted on wrestling matches, cock fights, and bear baiting.

YULETIDE FOOLS
One of the highlights of Christmas was the Feast of Fools. A "bishop" was chosen and dressed up in mock vestments. He led everyone into church and recited services in gibberish. Meanwhile, others played dice on the altar and sang rude songs.

BALANCING ACT
Acrobats, jugglers, and dancing bears were all popular forms of entertainment at medieval festivals.

THE GREAT FAIRS
Fairs often grew out of religious festivals. After Nôtre-Dame Cathedral in Paris acquired a piece of Christ's "true cross" in 1109, thousands of pilgrims came to visit this holy relic (p. 42) each June. Merchants set up their stalls in the surrounding streets, and soon the fair had grown into a major event. The Bishop of Paris is seen here bestowing a blessing on the proceedings.

FAIR CHEWS
There was plenty of food for sale at fairs and markets. Simple baked or deep-fried meat pies like these "chewets" were the most common fare.

OUT ON THE TOWN
Many people came to fairs simply to have a good time, and tavern keepers did a roaring trade. Large amounts of cheap ale and wine were consumed and drunkenness was common. In this Italian tavern, fresh quantities of wine are being passed up from the cellar to supply the carousing merchants.

Canvas
cover

New pattens
(p. 23) for sale

AT THE MARKET
Besides the great fairs,
there were weekly markets
in most big towns. Peddlers,
merchants, drovers of cattle,
sheep, pigs, and even geese,
all came. Stalls sold a huge
array of goods, from cheese,
eggs, and salt to pots and
pans, tools, knives, shoes,
and cloth. This reconstructed
medieval market stall
contains leather goods
that would have been
on sale at markets in the
14th and 15th centuries.

Large roll of
cattlehide

Wooden frame can
be easily folded up
for transporting
the stall

Leather
costrel
(p. 11)

Leather
tankards

Colored
goatskin
for making
shoes

Wooden shoe
"lasts" for
shoemaking

Leather
bottles

Old shoes waiting
to be mended

Leftover leather from
cut-out shoe patterns

Medieval music

In the Middle Ages, most people heard music in church. In the echoing spaces of the great cathedrals, monks and priests recited their texts by chanting them in a single key. This lovely form of singing was known as plainchant, or plainsong. Few cathedrals had organs, and church singing was usually unaccompanied by musical instruments, but kings and noblemen often dined to the sound of harps and lutes played by poet musicians called troubadours (p. 26). On feast days, ordinary people sang folk songs and danced to pipes and drums, and by 1400, most towns had a town band of professional musicians who accompanied processions with shawms (p. 58) and trumpets.

BEAR FOOT
Some musicians trained bears to dance and tumble to the music of the pipe and tabor. Bears were used because they could walk on two feet in a human way.

A MEDIEVAL DRUM KIT
Many musical instruments were brought to Europe by returning crusaders. These "nakers," or small drums (left), were modeled on the Middle Eastern *naqqara*, a kind of kettledrum with a curved body. Nakers were hung in pairs on a belt and usually played to accompany dance music.

Naker player

Hurdy-gurdy player

Turning the handle operates the instrument

The turning wheel plays the strings

FINE FIDDLE
Most troubadours in 13th-century France accompanied themselves on a fiddle. It was bigger than the modern violin and often rested in the lap. Only one string of this fiddle could be altered on the fingerboard. The other four were fixed strings that sounded a continuous bass tone, or drone.

SYMPHONY OF SOUND
Monks in 11th-century Spain used an *organistrum* to teach singing in their choir schools. This was a stringed instrument that needed two people to operate. One turned the handle while the other played the keys. The *organistrum* developed into the hurdy-gurdy, which could be played by one man. It could mingle several sounds together, so it came to be known as the "symphony."

Wheel cover

Drumstick

ONE-MAN BAND
The smallest of all dance bands
was the pipe and tabor. The
pipe had only three holes, and
the musician could easily play it
with his left hand while hitting the
tabor with his right. These simple
instruments were commonly used
to accompany village dances.

Bagpipe
player

*Sound comes out
through pipes*

Pipe

*The strings are
plucked with
goose quills*

*Snare adds
a buzz to
the sound of
the tabor*

*Musician blows
into mouthpiece
to inflate the bag*

HEAVENLY MUSIC
In medieval paintings, angels
were often shown playing the
psaltery, similar to a small harp.
It often formed part of a small
orchestra with other soft-toned
instruments such as the lute
(p. 44), viol, and flute.

*Pegs can be
tightened to
tune the
strings*

*Pipe is
played with
fingers*

*Outside strings
are bass strings,
or drones*

*Keys operate
the two inside
strings*

BAGPIPES
Contrary to legend, bagpipes
were not invented by the
Scots. In fact, in about 1300
they were being played in
many parts of the world,
including England, India,
and North Africa.

*Keys fall back
into place by
gravity*

*Bag is made
of leather*

Plays and parades

MEDIEVAL DRAMA was started by the Church. Sometime in the 11th century, priests began to add short scenes to the major religious services, such as those at Christmas and Easter. The scenes portrayed the great moments in the Bible – the fall of Adam, Noah escaping the flood, or Samson destroying the temple. People loved this new kind of entertainment. The scenes became so popular that they were performed in church porches, then on stages in town marketplaces, where more people could see them. By the 13th century, they had become complete cycles of plays, telling the whole Christian story and lasting as long as 40 days. In England, France, Italy, and Germany, they were staged by the local guilds (p. 50). They became known as "mystery" plays from the French word *metier*, or trade.

MASKS AND MUMMERS
Horses' heads, devil masks, drums, bells, and dances all played their part in a performance put on by mummers (above). On special occasions, mummers, or masked actors, staged short plays or mimes that told simple folktales, usually featuring dramatic sword fights and a doctor, who would enter at the end of the story and bring the dead back to life.

The dragon can be made to "breathe" fire and smoke by exploding small amounts of gunpowder inside its head

WILD GREEN MEN
Many pagan (non-Christian) rituals lived on in medieval Europe. Bands of "wodwos," or wild woodmen, dressed in leaves and greenery would rush into feasts and pageants, causing havoc. Their dances symbolized the untamed forces of nature. On the occasion shown above, their costumes accidentally caught fire from a candle!

FESTIVAL FANFARE
The shawm was a reed instrument with a loud, piercing sound that was played at town parades and festivals.

FUNNY FACE
In 1230, a priest complained of actors who "change and distort their bodies with shameful leaps and gestures." This stone carving shows a fool or jester literally "pulling a face" to amuse his audience. Fools also entertained people by telling rude jokes and waving a pig's bladder filled with dried peas.

PLAYING THE DEVIL
Like church carvings and stained glass windows (p. 34), mystery plays were a good way of teaching Bible stories to ordinary people who could not read and write. In this scene, the Devil is seen tempting Jesus in the wilderness. Each section of a mystery play was mounted on a wagon and drawn to a series of stations throughout the town. If spectators waited long enough in one spot, they would see the whole cycle of plays.

Carved wooden head decorated with bright paint

SNAP DRAGON
This wooden head belonged to a parade dragon that was used in processions to celebrate the feast day of St. George in the town of Norwich, England. It was operated by a man hidden inside the basketwork body and caused great amusement by snapping at the people who lined the streets. Dragons also played an important part in many mummers' plays, where they were usually shown battling with the valiant St. George.

The back of the dragon's head was fitted with a long wooden pole which was used for maneuvering the head

Lower jaw can be pulled up to make a snapping noise

Death and disease

DEATH WAS EVER-PRESENT for people living in the Middle Ages. Disease was rife in the dirty, overcrowded streets of medieval towns and cities, and medical knowledge was limited. The average life expectancy was about 30 years. Frequent wars and famines claimed thousands of lives at a time. The most catastrophic event of all was the Black Death. Carried by black rats, it was brought back from Asia by Italian sailors. The plague was deadly and highly contagious. Symptoms included black and blue blotches on the body. No cure was ever found. It swept through Europe between 1347 and 1350. By the end of 1348, at least a third of the entire population of Europe had died.

FEVERFEW
Strong-smelling feverfew was used to treat headaches and to assist in childbirth.

MARJORAM
Marjoram was used to make healing poultices to place on bruises and swellings.

LEMON BALM
This plant was seen as a kind of magic elixir that could cure serious illnesses. It was also used for fevers and colds because it causes sweating.

LUNGWORT
Because the shape of its leaves resembled lungs, lungwort was used to treat chest disorders.

HERBAL MEDICINE
Medieval medicine was based mainly on folklore and superstition rather than scientific observation. For example, many medical handbooks recommended that healing herbs should be picked on magical days of the year, such as Midsummer's Eve. However, many of the herbs used in medieval times are still employed by herbalists today.

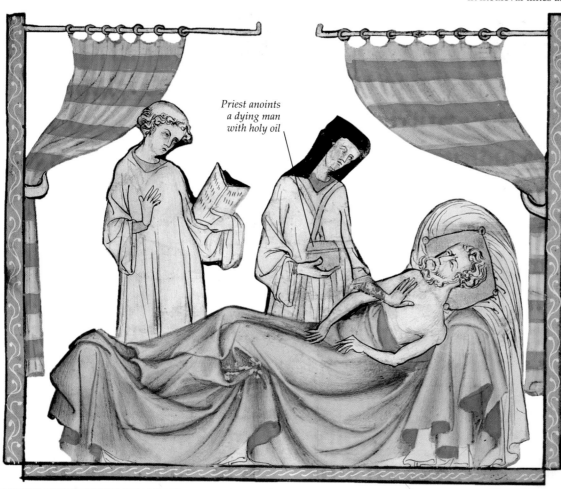

Priest anoints a dying man with holy oil

DOCTOR'S SURGERY
The most common form of surgery was bloodletting (above), which was carried out by uneducated barber-surgeons. People believed it restored the balance of the body's fluids, but more often it seriously weakened sick patients.

LAST RITES
People in the Middle Ages believed it was important to die properly. They thought that if they did not make a final confession of their sins to a priest, they would go to hell (p. 31). But as the Black Death raged, so many priests perished that most of the people who died were buried without prayers or ceremony.

Preparations were often stored in sheep's horns

Linen bung for powder container

Tooth powder was fairly abrasive

WORMWOOD
Wormwood was used to rid the digestive system of worms and was also placed in clothes to repel fleas.

Whelk shell

AT THE DENTIST
Without modern painkillers, most medieval surgical treatments must have been fairly unpleasant. Rotten teeth were yanked out by tooth pullers who worked at weekly markets.

Oyster shell

Cuttlefish

MEDIEVAL TOOTHPASTE
Ingredients like these were ground up to make powder for cleaning teeth. Such preparations would have been used by wealthy people mainly for cosmetic purposes, since there was no knowledge of the need for dental hygiene. Breath was sweetened with honey, and coriander or cumin seeds.

PLAGUE PITS
At the height of the Black Death, people had to carry their own dead to mass burial pits because there were not enough coffins to go round. In Paris nearly 800 people died every day. Simple lead crosses such as these were placed on the corpses.

Skeleton dances to a pipe and tabor (p. 57)

THE DANCE OF DEATH
The theme of death as the great leveler was acted out in the macabre Dance of Death. Men dressed as skeletons danced with figures representing each level of society to show that death comes to all. The Dance of Death was also depicted in many church carvings, paintings, and manuscripts.

Fearful monk is dragged off by the deathly dancer

FEAR OF THE PLAGUE
"This is the end of the world!" lamented an Italian chronicler of the Black Death. Many believed the plague was divine punishment for human sins, and the Church held special services and processions.

The birth of a new age

IN THE 15TH CENTURY, there was a rebirth, or renaissance, of interest in the arts and sciences. It began in Italy. The works of the great Latin and Greek writers were rediscovered and studied for the first time since the fall of Rome. They inspired artists and scholars to turn away from a strictly religious view of life and concentrate on human beings. Renaissance painters and sculptors began to explore the beauty of the human body, and poets wrote about human feelings and experiences. These new ideas also caused people to question traditional views on religion. Many thought that the Catholic Church (pp. 30–31) had become corrupt and needed change. A group of reformers called the Protestants rejected the authority of the Pope in Rome and set up new churches in northern Europe. This movement became known as the Reformation. It divided the Christian world and brought to an end the all-encompassing power of the medieval Church.

RELIGIOUS REFORMER
The religious Reformation was spearheaded by a German priest named Martin Luther (1483–1546). In 1517, he wrote a list of 95 arguments against Roman Catholic practices and nailed them to the door of Wittenberg Cathedral, provoking a wave of protest against the Church.

Hand-painted decoration

Gothic type imitates hand-written text

THE PRINTED WORD
Few inventions have changed the world as dramatically as the printing press. It was developed in Europe by Johannes Gutenberg (c. 1398–1468), who produced the first printed Bible in the 1450s. As printing techniques improved, books were produced more cheaply, encouraging the spread of learning.

PATRON OF PAINTERS
The Italian city of Florence was at the center of the artistic Renaissance. This was due largely to men such as Lorenzo de' Medici (1449–1492). Nicknamed "the Magnificent," he used his wealth to employ artists such as Michelangelo (p. 7).

NEW SCHOOLS
Before the Renaissance, nearly all schools were run by the Church. Afterward, many new grammar schools were founded by rich merchants and noblemen. The spread of education was hastened by the wider availability of books.

CONSTANTINOPLE FALLS
The Middle Ages ended as they began, with invaders from the East, this time the Ottoman Turks. In 1453, after a long siege, they conquered Constantinople, which became the Muslim city of Istanbul. It was the end of the thousand-year-old Christian Byzantine Empire in the East (p. 6).

RENAISSANCE MAN
Leonardo da Vinci (1452–1519) embodied the spirit of the Renaissance. He was a brilliant painter and sculptor who also had a keen interest in science, engineering, and architecture. His most famous painting is the *Mona Lisa*, but he also produced detailed anatomical drawings and sketches for numerous inventions, such as this flying machine.

NEW FIRE POWER
The development of guns made an enormous difference to warfare after the mid-14th century. Cannons could break down castle walls, and bullets could pierce metal armor, bringing an end to the era of the medieval knight.

THE GREAT NAVIGATORS
In the 15th century, Europeans embarked on great voyages of discovery as they searched for sea routes to Asia. From the 1420s, Portuguese sailors ventured down the long west coast of Africa in caravels like this one. In 1488, Bartholomew Diaz rounded the Cape of Good Hope and sailed into the Indian Ocean for the first time. By 1498, Vasco da Gama had reached India. Meanwhile, Christopher Columbus crossed the Atlantic in 1492 and claimed America for the Spanish king.

Index

Acknowledgments

Dorling Kindersley would like to thank:
The York Archaeological Trust for Excavation and Research Ltd; Richard Fitch and Mark Meltonville of Wolfbane; Peter and Joyce Butler, and Tracy Chadwick (medical herbalist) of Saxon Village Crafts; Anthony Barton, medieval musical instrument consultant; Bob Powell at the Weald and Downland Open Air Museum, Sussex; Steve Hollick and Chris Kemp, and all members of the National Guild of Stonemasons and Carvers, London; Caroline Benyon at Carl Edwards Studio; the Department of Medieval and Later Antiquities at the British Museum, London; the Museum of London; Jon Marrow at Norton Priory Museum Trust; the Dean and Chapter of York; All Saints Church, North Street, York; St Nicholas Church, Stanford-on-Avon; Castle Museum Norwich, Norfolk Museums Service; Susila Baybars for editorial help; Joe Hoyle and Cormac Jordan for design help.
Additional photography by Peter Anderson (40bc, 49cl, 52c,bl, 55c, 60tr, 61tr); John Chase (42cr, 46–47, 61cl);

Andy Crawford (54bl); Steve Gorton (19tr, 32–33c); Peter Hayman, Ivor Kerslake, and Nick Nichols (22cr, 30c,l, 31bl, 42cl,bc); Gary Ombler (38–39);
Model by Peter Griffiths (32–33)
Artworks by Anna Ravenscroft (40);
John Woodcock (52–53)
Endpapers by David Graham
Picture credits
a=above, b=below, c=center, l=left, r=right, t=top
AKG, London: 6br, 38bc, 61br, 62bl; /Photo: Erich Lessing/San Apollinare in Classe, Ravenna: 6lc /Photo: Erich Lessing /Galleria dell'Accademia, Florence: 7rc /Pfarrkirche, Cappenberg: 7bl; /Nuremburg City Library: 19tl; /Bern, Burgerbibliotheque: 21tl; /Bibliotheque de Ste Genevieve: 31tl; /Bibliotheque Nationale, Paris: 48tr, 56tr, 61tc, 63tr; Ancient Art & Architecture Collection: 25bl, 32tr; Musee des Arts Decoratifs, Paris/Photo: Sully-Jaulmes: 14c; Ashmolean Museum, Oxford: 7c, 45bl; Keith Barley: 35tl; Bridgeman Art Library, London: /Bibliotheque de la Sorbonne, Paris: 6bl; /Trinity College,

Dublin: 6tr; /British Library, London: 7tc, 9br, 10br, 10bl, 12br, 14cl, 15bl, 20tr, 22cl, 23cl, 24br, 30tl, 31tr, 36b &c, 42br, 43cl, 45cl, 50br, 50cl, 51cl, 54br, 58c, 60br, Front Jacket: lc & tl, Back Jacket: lac, bl, b, tc, rbc, Inside front flap; /With special authorisation of the City of Bayeux: 7tl; /Victoria & Albert Museum, London: 8tr; /Musee Condee, Chantilly /Giraudon: 12tr, 17tr, 30bc, 60bl; /Vatican Library, Rome: 15tl; /Fitzwilliam Museum, University of Cambridge: 15cl, 27bl, Back Jacket: tc; /Bibliotheque Nationale, Paris: 22tr, 27tl, 28tr, 44tr, 45cr, 54c, Back Jacket: tr; /Kunsthistorisches Museum, Vienna: 24bc; /Department of the Environment, London: 25tl; /Westminster Abbey, London: 26tr; /Sixt Parish Church, Haut-Savoie, France: 31br; /Galleria degli Uffizi, Florence: 35br; /San Francesco Upper Church, Assisi: 37tl; /Seminario Patriarcale, Venice: 47bl; /Staatsarchiv, Hamburg: 47tc; /British Museum: 48bl; /Bibliotheque Royale de Belgique, Brussels: 48c; /City of Bristol Museum & Art Gallery: 62tl; /Bibliotheque de l'Institut de France, Paris /Giraudon: 63tl; British Library, London: 53br, 54cr, 54tl, 56c, 62c, Front Jacket: bcr; British Museum, London: 27r, 30bl, 45tr, Back Jacket: lc; Jean-Loup Charmet: 41tl, 42tr; Musee de

Cluny, Paris: 62bc; Danish National Museum, Copenhagen: 6c; E.T. Archive, London: 24ac, 29cc, 34tl; /Victoria & Albert Museum, London: 11br, 11cr, 16tl; /British Library, London: 14tr; /Biblioteca Marciana: 22bl; /Bibliotheque Nationale, Paris: 28cl; /Biblioteca Estense, Modena: 38c; /Collegio del Cambio, Perugia: 46cl; /Biblioteca Augustea, Perugia: 53tr; Mary Evans Picture Library, London: 24tr; Werner Forman Archive, London; /Metropolitan Museum of Art, New York: 45br; Photographie, Giraudon /Bibliotheque Nationale, Paris: 8tl; Sonia Halliday & Laura Lushington Photographs /Victoria & Albert Museum, London: 12c ; Sonia Halliday Photographs: 35c, 58tr; Robert Harding Picture Library: 7br, 26br, 33tl, 40br, 51tl, 56bl; Michael Holford: 14bl; Museum of London: 52bc; Puffin Books: Churches & Cathedrals by Helen Leacroft, 1957. Reproduced by permission of Penguin Books Ltd: 33tl, 33cr; Scala, Florence: /Archivo di Stato, Siena: 8lc; /Museo dell'Opera del Duomo, Orvieto: 50tl, 50bl, 51br, 51tl; Sir John Soane's Museum, London: 33br; Trinity College Library, Cambridge: 39tr; Wallace Collection: 25tr, 49tl; Woodmansterne: 61bl; Zefa Pictures: 48br.

Conard High School Library

West Hartford, Conn.

DATE DUE

RR   Langley, Andrew
940.1   Medieval Life
LAN

101919